TALKING TO
HENRY

and other short stories

CYNTHIA TUCK

With love to Wendy
from Cynthia
Dec '07

© Cynthia Tuck 2007
Talking to Henry

ISBN: 978-0-9557782-0-9

Published by
Yellow Door Press
5 Heathfield Close
Midhurst
West Sussex
GU29 9PS

A CIP catalogue record of this book
can be obtained from the British Library.

Book designed by
RPM Print & Design
2-3 Spur Road
Chichester
West Sussex
PO19 8PR

CONTENTS

For George

1 ~ Talking to Henry

'I don't think I'll go to Guy's wedding, Henry,' said Jane, 'I've always been fond of Guy, but it's a long way to go, and weddings are for the young and not for old fogies like me. I wonder what his Fiona is like – he has never brought her to meet me?'

Henry did not answer. Henry never did – because Henry was a china ornament which sat on Jane's mantelpiece. He came to her, together with a collection of other somewhat eccentric ornaments after her equally eccentric Cousin Cedric had died. Henry was a strange bird. He would baffle any ornithologist. He was settled on a round base, and his body rose straight from one five-clawed foot and was topped by a big head with a large beak. One eye was winking and the other, Jane was sure, twinkled. He was designed as some kind of storage jar and his strange head was detachable – but Jane never detached it. Living alone, Jane often talked to him, mostly to consolidate her thoughts and to hear her own voice – and she found the conspiratorial twinkle in his eye friendly and cheerful.

Jane's conversation with Henry was terminated by a 'Coo-ee!' from the back door.

It was her friend Dorothy and soon they were enjoying coffee and home-made biscuits together.

'I do love your cottage, Jane,' Dorothy said, 'It is so pretty and cosy.'

'I know,' said Jane offering her friend another biscuit, 'but several problems have unearthed themselves lately. Apart from the fact that the cottage really needs re-thatching, I have damp coming up one of the walls in the kitchen, the wiring must be due for some sort of overhaul and the outside paintwork badly needs attention.'

'Oh dear!' Dorothy grimaced sympathetically. 'These things are so expensive to get done.'

'That's certainly true – I have had one or two quotes. I am beginning to think that perhaps the sensible thing to do would be to sell the cottage and find something which I could better afford to keep up. I hear that a small block of flats may be built in Sommerton – that's not too far away.'

'But you would so miss your cottage and its little garden – and the village.' Dorothy said sadly.

'Yes, I know – we came here when Jack retired and we were always so happy here, but since he died of course my financial situation has changed. I didn't worry too much about the cottage at first and I couldn't have entertained the thought of moving – but during the last year or so I realise that it will deteriorate unless it has money spent on it – more money than I can manage to find. So I must be realistic about it. Have another cup of coffee?'

'Thank you,' said Dorothy, 'and then I must get off to the village shop.'

When Dorothy left Jane closed the front door and went over to the mantelpiece.

'Well Henry – I've said it out loud. I've said that perhaps I ought to sell the cottage. I said it to Dorothy – well, you heard me. I'm probably right. We'll have to see - in the spring, perhaps. And the other thing, Henry, is that I think that I'll give you to Guy and his Fiona as a wedding present. Guy always liked you, ever since he used to come and see us when he was a little boy. I'm sure he'll be pleased to have you as his own. I haven't got to take any notice of that awfully impersonal present list they sent.'

So the next day Jane washed Henry carefully and wrapped him up in an ocean of bubble wrap. 'I shall miss you, Henry,' she said, as she gently placed him in a nice sturdy box, 'but I'm sure you'll be happy with Guy.' She took the parcel to the Post Office, where Mrs Curtis stuck 'Fragile with Care' stickers on it. And off went Henry.

* * * * *

The following Saturday morning a loud banging on the door of Guy's flat heralded the arrival of the parcel. Guy carried it into the living room where Fiona had arrived to discuss the seating plan for the wedding reception. Papers were strewn all over the table and the parcel was plonked unceremoniously on top of them and Fiona proceeded to open it. Out of the bubble wrap peeped a huge beak and a winking eye.

'What the hell is this?' she shrieked as she extricated Henry from the bubble wrap, 'what a simply hideous thing!'

'Oh!' exclaimed Guy, 'its Henry!'

'Who or what is Henry – apart, that is, from some sort of ornament in simply appalling taste?'

'He's from Aunt Jane – my grandmother's younger sister who lives in Kent. Yes – here's a card from her. She says that she can't come to the wedding but sends her very best wishes and thought that we would like Henry because I used to like him when I came to her house – how kind of her.'

'If you expect me to live with that ghastly creature, Aunt Jane or not – you've got another think coming!' snorted Fiona.

'Love me, love Henry!' said Guy, playfully slapping her bottom.

* * * * *

One day some months later Jane and Dorothy had been looking at flats for some of the morning and for most of the afternoon.

'What an exhausting business!' sighed Jane. 'Shoes off and kettle on!'

'A cup of tea would be like nectar!' said Dorothy as she flopped down into a chair.

'How many flats do you think we have seen ?'

'Seems like a hundred,' answered Jane, raising her voice over the noise of water gushing into the kettle, ' Thank you so much for coming with me. We seem to have covered quite a wide area. I'm afraid that I didn't really like any of them very much – and I would so like to stay in the village. But I must do something fairly soon as the agent says that it would be *a good time* to put the cottage on the market.'

'But that's the sort of thing the agent would say – don't let them rush you. You don't want to be forced into buying something in a hurry,' warned her friend.

'That's true. Oh Dorothy – I'm hating the thought of selling the cottage.'

'I know you are, dear. And so am I – it won't feel right here without you in this cottage.'

As they sat gratefully drinking their tea Dorothy said, 'Daughter Jenny rang last night – she wants me to stay in London for a few days the week after next.'

'That will be nice Dorothy. How are they all?'

'They seem fine – busy of course. At least I'll be able to help with the children a bit . It will be lovely to be with them.'

Then Dorothy looked up at the mantelpiece. 'Your mantelpiece looks strange without Henry sitting there winking.'

'Yes I know,' answered her friend, 'its ridiculous, but I really do miss him – I often used to talk to him. I think that Cousin Cedric did, too. 'You silly funny old bird!' he used to say to him. I was very fond of Cousin Cedric. He 'collected' things – he left me several boxes of bits and pieces which are up in the attic – I must see if I can find something else to replace Henry on the mantelpiece. I hope that Guy and his wife are enjoying him.'

* * * * *

Alas, however, Guy and Fiona's enjoyment of Henry was not at all mutual. Fiona, slouching about in her dressing gown this particular morning, peered almost malevolently at Henry. He was sitting on a shelf mostly hidden from view by an ornament she considered to be in much better taste. She hated Henry's winking eye, his silly beaked face and his five-clawed foot. She was unhappy and discontented in the flat. She had hoped that they would have been in a position to buy a house soon after they were married. Guy had said that they would be able to, but now seemed to be getting cold feet about it.

The phone rang. It was her mother, who wanted to know if she had remembered about the charity jumble sale this morning and was she coming to help?

Fiona lied about not remembering, said she was coming and hastily shovelled herself into some jeans and a sweat shirt. The last thing she did before she left the flat was defiantly to grab Henry from his perch and bundle him into a plastic bag.

Mrs Pearson, the headmaster's wife, was manning the white elephant stall at the jumble sale. She wondered how ever she was going to sell even a fraction of the motley collection of people's cast off possessions which were festooned on the large trestle table over which she was presiding. Mr Harvey from the local antique shop opened the proceedings in great style and the waiting queue swarmed in. Mr Harvey himself came straight over to Mrs Pearson's stall.

'Morning Mrs Pearson!' he said cheerfully, casting an expert eye over her wares, 'what treasures have we here then?'

'As you see,' she smiled, 'treasures galore!'

Mr Harvey's eyes narrowed as they quickly alighted on Henry.

'Here's a strange fellow!' he said, turning Henry upside down, ' not to too many people's taste I think! Never mind – I'll give you a fiver for him to start you off.'

'Thank you Mr Harvey, that is very generous of you!' Mrs Pearson said as she happily put the five pound note in her tin, 'I was going to suggest £1! Would you like this plastic bag?'

* * * * *

In the room at the back of his shop, Mr Harvey was on the telephone.

'Frazer Antiques and Ceramics,' said an answering voice.

'Is that you, Marcus?'

'Speaking.'

'Charles Harvey, Marcus. Dorchester.'

'Oh, hello Charlie! How's life treating you?'

'Medium, medium. Trade's not all that brisk.'

'We all say that Charlie – like the farmers grumbling about the weather! What can I do for you old man?'

'Well, it so happened that I was offered a genuine Wallace Martin Wally bird – couldn't resist it – ended up paying well over the original asking price, mind you. I'll have no trouble selling it on, but I thought of you – don't I remember you saying that you've a customer keen to buy into this field? Would you like first refusal?'

'Mmm – American couple. What size is this Wally Bird?'

'15 inches – I'm still in English – that'd be about 40cms. It's a storage version. Detachable head. Probably for tobacco. Absolutely perfect condition.'

'Factory mark?'

'Wallace Martin Bros. London and Southall. Date mark is 5:1899. Are you interested?'

'Hmm – what sort of money are we talking about?'

'Six Grand.'

'You'll have to come down from that a bit Charlie – can't set myself up as a philanthropic society. Anyway, I can't say any more until I see it.'

'It'd go for more than that at auction, Howard. It's a good price – it's a real beauty. Anyway, I'm coming to London next week and I'll bring it in if you're interested.'

'OK. Do that.'

'Right. I'll be in touch. Cheerio Howard.'

Mr Harvey put the phone down on his dusty desk and smiled.

* * * * *

A week or so later a plump American gentleman followed by his equally plump wife entered the Frazer Antiques and Ceramics shop in the Kings Road.

'Ah! – Mr and Mrs Coogan – how nice to see you!' greeted the proprietor, hand outstretched.

'Hi. Mr Frazer!' beamed Mrs Coogan, 'We were interested when you called us about the Wally bird – weren't we, Wilmer?'

'Sure were!' agreed her husband.

Mr Frazer gave a professional smile, 'I had considerable difficulty in tracking one down – they are very much sought after by collectors. However, I have managed to find a particularly fine example. Perhaps you would like to come through and have a look at it? Malcolm! Come and take over in the shop please.'

Mr Frazer led his clients through into a smaller room where Henry was perched on a table looking knowing and quite bizarre.

'Isn't he fine?' said Mr Frazer, 'and in absolutely perfect condition.'

'Ooh Wilmer!' Mrs Coogan squealed, 'Isn't he just cute? He's got such a wicked expression! And look – his head comes off!'

'Probably intended originally to store tobacco,' volunteered Mr Frazer.

Mr Coogan took Henry carefully in his plump hands. 'He's a great example of English eccentricity,' he said. 'What date do you reckon?'

'It has it on the bottom – 1899, and even the month that it was fired, and it is marked Wallace Martin and Bros. London and Southall.'

'Is Southall in the North Country?' Mrs Coogan wanted to know.

'No, its now a suburb of London. But when the factory was built in the 1870's it was probably quite rural.'

'I guess you wouldn't mind if I just had a look at it through my magnifying glass?' asked Mr Coogan.

'Of course not, go ahead.'

Mr Coogan peered at Henry carefully. 'Mmm – can't see any damage or signs of repair.'

'Would you like a look, honey?'

'Seems just fine to me,' said his wife, 'do you think we could have him Wilmer darling?'

'Now hang on a minute – we haven't talked money with Mr Frazer yet. How much are we looking at here?'

'£7,750.'

' Pounds or dollars?'

'Pounds.'

Mr Coogan whistled. 'That much?'

'It would cost you more than that if you bought it at auction. These pieces are becoming very rare nowadays – especially in perfect condition. They are all very individually made and are real collectors items. The birds were all made by the brother called Wallace, who was the modeller – hence the name Wally birds.'

Mr Coogan was pondering. '£7,250?' he bargained.

'I couldn't take any less than £7,500 and that is only because you are a valued customer.'

Mr Coogan considered for a while, pursing his lips and looking quizzically at Henry.

Eventually he said, 'OK. Done! I'll give my bank a call.'

'Thank you Mr Coogan,' responded MrFrazer, picking up Henry with a satisfied smile.

'I'll just ask Malcolm to pack it up very carefully for you. You've got a rare bird here! Please excuse me.'

Mrs Coogan clutched her husband's arm. 'Oh Wilmer – isn't it exciting? Wait till our friends in the States see him when we get back next year! He'll be a real star in our collection!'

'Yeah,' responded her husband, 'and a darned expensive one, too. Thank goodness we have gotten that new burglar alarm fixed up.'

* * * * *

A car glided past the expensive houses in a West Hampstead street, and came to a stop as its lights were turned off. Inside were two men in dark overalls.

'OK. Mick,' whispered one, 'this'll do fine. Nice quiet dark road and 'ouses spread apart like.'

'China job din't yer say Joe? I got all the wraps 'ere.'

'Yeah, that's right, thanks mate.'

The two men slipped out of the car and like the professionals they were, moved quickly and silently over the front lawn to the house, continuing their whispered conversation.

'Nah,' said Joe, 'the boss an' I 'did a really good recky rahned this place last week. We garbed up in those telephone overalls wot ole Fred got us, waited for the gaffa and his missus to go aht, banged on the door an' said that someone 'ad reported the phone aht o'rorder. The cleaning lady fell for it – no trubs. So we went all over the joint, fiddlin' wiv the phones and said we fixed it fine. Mrs Mop even made us a cuppa tea!' he grinned widely.

'We worked out how to shut the alarm off – the lot.'

'You sure these guys are away an' not just aht for the evening?' queried Mick.

'Yeah, positive. They went away s'mornin with cases and stuff. The boss watched 'em from the top of the road. He sat in'is smart car reading a posh newspaper.'

By now they had sidled round to the side of the house.

'I'm gunna get in thru this side wnda' wot I know aint wired up,' said Joe, 'I'll sort the alarm then let you in thru' the front door – jus like a gent. OK.?

Like quicksilver the two men were inside the house.

'Where's the stuff?' whispered Mick.

'Room at the back 'ere. Proper contract job this. No electric gear, no sparklers – jus' everything in these two 'ere cabinets. I'll take this' un an 'you do that. Plenty o' wraps mind, some o' these things look right delicate – no good to the boss if they're broke.'

Swiftly and deftly they got to work and soon the cabinets were empty.

'Cor!, said Mick,' look at this bird thing over 'ere – want 'im?'

'Yeah – shove 'im in – and those coupla vases an' stuff. We can take the rubbish things to Pete in the Portobello. Bound to be worth summat.'

In about ten minutes after their arrival the operation was over and Joe and Mick were driving quietly away.

* * * * *

On the Sunday morning they were in the Portobello Road.

'Ere's Pete's pad,' said Joe. 'Can't see Pete.'

'I think that's 'is lad at the stall,' said Mick, 'I'll 'ave a word wiv 'im. Hey, son, is the gaffa around?'

'Me Dad? No – 'e's 'avin some liquid refreshment. I'm lookin' after things 'ere. Can I 'elp ya?'

'We've jus' got a few things 'ere that 'e may be int'rested to shift. We'll prob'ly see 'im in the pub. Is it OK. if we jus' leave 'em down 'ere in the box for now – there's nuffin worth much. We'll go an' 'ave a coupla beers an' come back later.'

'What's yer names – to tell me Dad?'

'Joe an' Mick. See ya later.'

'OK! said Pete's lad, 'Cheers!'

Joe and Mick disappeared into the browsing crowd and the lad thought he would see what was in the box they had left. The first thing he took out, wrapped up in newspaper, was Henry, as Henry had been almost sticking out of the box. 'Blimey!' muttered the boy aloud.' What an ugly devil – never seen one o' these 'afore! Shouldn't think this'll go for much.'

Farther down Portobello Jane's friend Dorothy and her daughter Jenny were having a leisurely amble around the stalls.

'I haven't been to the Portobello Road for years,' Dorothy was saying, 'Its good of Martin to look after the children and give us a morning to ourselves.'

'Its certainly better coming here without a baby buggy and a toddler,' smiled Jenny, 'I love it here – all the hub-bub and the characters – let alone the amazing collection of things on the stalls. There's some awful rubbish, but you can get some bargains. Looking for anything special, Mum?'

'No dear, just browsing. Your father will thank me for leaving everything here exactly where it is!'

The colourful noisy scene swirled around them – vendors were shouting and punters were bargaining; silver was gleaming and clothes dangling; there was bric-a-bac galore and stalls piled with old unattractive items all described as 'antiques'. There were also some very desirable real antique pieces of furniture, jewellery and china. It was lovely and busy and fun and Dorothy was enjoying it immensely. Suddenly she clutched Jenny's arm.

'Oh, look! There's a Henry!'

'Henry who?' asked Jenny in surprise.

'Not a Henry person, a Henry bird.'

'Mum, whatever are you talking about? What is a Henry bird for goodness sake?'

'On that stall over there – in that lad's hand – that china bird!'

'Better go over and see – he seems to be taking its head off.'

They hustled their way through the crowd to the stall where the teenaged boy was looking at Henry extremely dubiously.

'Excuse me,' Dorothy said to him, 'could I please have a look at that?'

The boy looked up and grinned. 'This bird Luv? Sure! Handsome fellow ain't he? Very – er – different sorta piece this.'

'Is it undamaged? asked Dorothy, inspecting Henry carefully.

'Perfect condition, lady.' This statement was rather surprisingly true.

'How much are you asking for him?' enquired Dorothy.

The boy thought quickly and took a chance on £25.

'Won't you take any less than that?' said Dorothy – she was after all, in the Portobello Road.

'OK. – £20 – but I hope me dad don' find out – he don' like me nearly givin' the stock away.'

'All right, I'll take it for £20,' said Dorothy, extricating a note from her purse, 'thank you very much.'

'Righto! got yerself a bargain luv. There y'go!'

Once more Henry was bundled into a plastic bag, and the young vendor thought how pleased his father would be when he told him that he had sold a real rubbish-looking ornament for £20.

As they left the stall Jenny said 'Oh Mum! Whatever have you bought that funny bird for? Whatever is Dad going to say to that?'

'It's not for me, but for Jane,' Dorothy said and proceeded to explain about Henry to Jenny. 'This bird looks identical to her other Henry.'

I expect that they stamped hundreds out the same. Can't say that I've noticed any, though – probably because I would hardly have coveted one if I had!'

'Anyway, I'm sure that Jane will be pleased to have a replacement for her Henry – she was only saying the other day that she was missing him. So I just couldn't resist buying this one. How amazing that I happened to see it!'

'Yes it was,' Jenny agreed, 'Its sad that she feels that she must sell her sweet cottage.'

'I know,' said Dorothy. 'As soon as I get back I shall give her this – it may cheer her up a little. Oh. look! – Laura would love one of those pink and white cuddly bunnies over there. Her birthday is soon – shall I buy her one?'

'That would be lovely! Then we must get back and relieve Martin of his bout of intensive fatherhood.'

* * * * *

Jane was making pastry when the door bell rang. She wiped her hands quickly on the nearest tea towel and still dripping pastry, answered the door. It was Dorothy, clutching a strange-shaped parcel.

'Dorothy, – how nice to see you! Time for a cup of coffee?' Have you had a good time in London?'

'I have, I have!' said Dorothy stepping inside, 'and I have brought you a present.' She thrust the parcel into Jane's hands.

'Dorothy, whatever is this?' Jane said, fumbling with wrapping papers. 'Oh, my goodness – its Henry!!'

'Well, it can't be your real Henry – I found him on the Portobello Road when I was in London with Jenny.'

'But he looks *exactly* the same! Oh Dorothy – thank you so much – how very kind of you,' Jane said, kissing her friend and then kissing Henry.

'I knew you were missing Henry and I just couldn't resist getting this one when I saw him. Jenny said that most probably lots were stamped out at the time and so they would all look the same.

'I suppose so,' smiled Jane, 'anyway, I'm delighted with him. Now, as the sun has gone over the yard arm as Jack used to say, let's have something to drink a bit stronger than coffee.'

After Dorothy had left Jane carefully washed her new rather grubby-looking Henry and took him over to the mantelpiece. She replaced an odd-looking owl which she had found in one of Uncle Cedric's boxes with Henry Mark 2, and looked at him with satisfaction. 'There', she said to him, 'I don't know how many of you there are, but I shall love you like my other Henry, because I certainly could not tell you apart – and you are winking at me, just the same as he did.'

* * * * *

Guy arrived back in the flat tired and disgruntled. He dumped his briefcase and jacket down in the hall and slumped into an armchair in the living room. Fiona emerged from the bedroom. 'Oh, hello,' she said, looking at her husband without much enthusiasm, 'had a good trip to Manchester?'

'Not specially,' was the reply. 'Business is not all that good at the moment and the journey was a nightmare.'

'Oh dear,' responded Fiona, 'now if you had got that nice little job in The City, you probably wouldn't have to travel to places like Manchester – and you'd be earning more money.'

'Don't bring up that old chestnut again – I didn't get that 'nice little job in The City' and I'm tired and hungry. I'll get myself a drink. Like one?'

'Yes please.'

Guy poured them each a drink. 'Well, its our first anniversary weekend. Here's to us!' he said, slumping back in his chair and gulping at his drink. 'What are we going to do this weekend?'

'Well,' said Fiona, pursing her lips, 'I thought that we could take Mummy and Daddy out for a meal at The Majestic.'

'That'd cost an arm and a leg!' protested Guy.

'Oh darling, don't be mean – it is special and The Majestic is *the* place to go.'

Guy sighed. 'Yes I know – I expect we can manage it – but we are not all that flush for money at the moment – we seem to have spent a hell of a a lot this year.'

'Are you trying to tell me that I'm extravagant?' Fiona's voice went up a couple of pitches. 'You can't expect me to slum it – love in a garret and all that sort of thing!'

Guy glared at his petulant partner. 'Fiona, we are nowhere near 'slumming it' – we don't live in a garret, we have a perfectly OK. flat.'

'I'm sorry Guy – its just that I feel claustrophobic here. It would be so nice to have a house and more space for entertaining, so that we can ask all the right sort of people.'

'The 'right sort of people' as far as I'm concerned,' retorted Guy, 'would be happy to have a meal with us wherever we may live. We shall be able to look for a house when we have a bit more capital – which at this rate is hardly piling up very quickly. We either economise or stay here longer – you can't have it both ways. 'Cut your coat according to your cloth' my father always said.'

'But I want lots of cloth, and a simply beautiful coat!' wheedled Fiona.

'You'll just have to wait, then,' Guy said impatiently, 'meantime, is there any chance of some supper?'

'Yes, I've got a couple of take-away pizzas. I've been shopping all day with Araminta and haven't had time to cook.'

'Good job that 'the right sort of people' aren't coming to supper tonight, then! While you are using all your ingenuity taking the pizzas out of their packets and putting them in the microwave, I'll put my feet up and finish my drink. Perhaps there's something interesting on the box.'

Fiona flounced out to the kitchen and Guy reached for the television remote control and watched as the screen came to life.

'That item about Staffordshire figurines almost brings to an end this week's 'Talking About Antiques,' the presenter was saying, 'but our ceramics expert Harold Witherspoon has just one more thing to show us. Harold ...'

The camera turned to a man with an egg-bald head who was clasping a china creature which looked a bit like Henry. Guy jerked up in his chair, spilling his drink.

'Now here is a strange fellow,' Mr Witherspoon expounded, 'he is a Wally Bird. Made by Wallace Martin of the Martin Brothers who had a factory at Southall, Middlesex for quite a long period around the turn of the century. Wallace was the modeller and he designed each piece individually. An ornithologist's nightmare but a collector's delight, these birds are highly sought after and not easy to come by. Copies have been made, but any genuine piece has an authentic mark on the bottom and the month and year of manufacture' Here he turned the creature ignominiously upside down and the camera zoomed in to the marking. 'Of special interest are the larger versions with removable heads which were often used to store tobacco. A piece such as that in good condition would sell for £8 – £10, 000 at auction.'

Guy ceased to listen. His eyes were popping out of his head. He looked up at the shelf where Henry had stood behind another ornament, to note that Fiona must have moved him.

'Fiona!' he yelled, leaping out of his chair, 'where is that bird ornament that Aunt Jane gave us? Fiona! Feeeona!'

* * * * *

Jane's telephone shrilled. 'Hello, hello!' she answered to an excited Dorothy at the other end.

'Jane! Jane! Have you been watching the antiques' programme on the tele – and the bit at the end about the Wally Birds – just like Henry?!'

'Yes I have!' laughed Jane, 'I feel almost speechless! I was going to phone you when I got my breath back. Henry certainly has the right sort of maker's marks.'

'It seems that these Henrys of yours have been hiding quite a secret. 'Wally Bird' doesn't seem a very appropriate name for them.'

'Hence the knowing cheeky look perhaps?' answered Jane. 'Wily' would be better!'

'Anyway,' continued her friend, 'if Henry really is worth a lot of money and you sold him that would help towards some repairs to your cottage?'

'Oh no dear, I would not sell him.'

'You wouldn't? Why not?'

'Well you see, when I went up to the attic to look for something to put in Henry's place, I started looking carefully in Uncle Cedric's boxes – which I never really had time to do before. When I said that Uncle Cedric collected things, I really didn't know the half of it – there are all sorts of weird and wonderful china things in the boxes – including *several* more Wally-like birds!' I had no idea, of course, that they were of such value – and I didn't like them much – but Henry came out of the box because he had such a cheeky face, and I was very fond of Cousin Cedric – he used to make me laugh and laugh – so Henry always reminds me of him.'

'Oh Jane, this is wonderful!' Dorothy's voice came so loudly down the phone that Jane had to move the handset away from her ear, 'it could all be out of a story!'

'Yes it could. I shall get them valued professionally as soon as possible and it would be lovely if I could stay in my cottage after all, if they raise enough money. But I shall certainly never part with Henry now! But you, Dorothy, must have a share in my good fortune, as if it wasn't for you I wouldn't have a Henry back. and I may never have realized that I have a few thousand pounds sitting in the attic!'

'But I am so delighted about the whole thing,' said Dorothy, brushing Jane's last remark aside, 'I shall phone Jenny now as she was with me when I bought Henry and I think she thought that I was a bit potty! Anyway, keep me in touch with developments, and Good Luck!'

'Thank you Dorothy. Thanks for everything!'

Jane put the phone down and walked over to the mantelpiece. 'Now Henry, you wily old bird, what have you been up to?' she said, stroking his overlarge beak, 'I have an uncanny feeling that you <u>are</u> my same old Henry – especially as you are said to be all so individual. Only you know how you have come back to me. I'm going to let you keep your secrets – it may well be unwise and not very tactful to probe into them. Let sleeping birds lie! Anyway, its lovely to have you back and hopefully we will stay together now, in this cottage, with happy memories of Jack and love and thanks to Cousin Cedric.'

She paused, about to turn away. 'Henry!' she said, smiling, 'are you winking at me?'

2 ~ A Silent Response

The beautiful naked girl who was draped on the two-seater settee shivered. There was a camera flash. And then another.

'I'm getting cold,' the girl complained, 'haven't you taken enough yet?'

'Just two more Lorna honey, and that'll be fine,' answered the photographer, 'you've been very patient – don't you think so, Giles?'

The sculptor, feasting his eyes on the wonderfully made body of the girl and imagining her softly rounded curves and her delicate features already immortalized in marble, agreed. 'You've been great, Lorna. Sorry about the temperature – I thought I turned the heating up as far as I could. Can you just move your head up a fraction more for the last couple of shots? That's it – perfect!'

The camera flashed two or three times more and then the girl hopped down from the settee and scuttled behind a screen to dress. She soon emerged in jeans and a large blue sweater.

'Thanks a lot, Lorna,' smiled Giles, 'I may need you once or twice more. A cheque will be in the post.'

'And I shall expect myself to be in a top gallery somewhere - eventually!'

'The next Summer Exhibition is my dream,' said Giles.

'Dream on then!' She blew a kiss to them both and let herself out of the studio door.

The photographer started packing up his equipment. 'She's certainly lovely, Guy. Where did you find her?'

'Through a rather up-market agency. She didn't really want to sit naked – but she was worth persuading! I think that you got the lighting just right. I shall have to think very hard about what pose to choose – perhaps the marble will tell me.'

'Life size?'

'No, 60% I think – more delicate.'

Further discussion was cut short as the door of the studio burst open, heralding the arrival of Rowena, her purple coat swirling about her.

'Oh hello darling,' said Giles, 'I didn't expect you.'

'I don't imagine you did – and who was that little tart who was leaving just as I was parking the car?'

'That wasn't a little tart, it was my new model – and this, as you know, is Stuart, who I asked to come along and take some photographs.'

'Oh, hello Stuart – I hope you've had a very enjoyable afternoon,' Rowena sneered.

'Mm, yes,' mumbled Stuart, shovelling himself into his jacket and picking up an armful of equipment.

'I'll help you to the car with your gear,' Giles said.

'Thanks. 'Bye, Rowena!'

Rowena did not bother to answer.

The two men stacked Stuart's equipment in his car. Giles said apologetically, somewhat embarrassed, 'I'm sorry about Rowena being rather rude like that.'

'That's OK – she's your problem rather than mine.'

'True. Things aren't going very well between us these days. She has become an insanely jealous woman, and she has nothing to be jealous about. I hate arguing and quarrelling.'

'Probably her time of life,' Stuart said as he got into his car, ' – women get less attractive and we chaps get more attractive.'

Giles laughed. 'Speak for yourself!' he said, as Stuart drove off.

Returning to the studio Giles said quietly to Rowena, 'There was no need to be unpleasant in front of Stuart.'

'What do you mean, be unpleasant! There you both were, incarcerated with a little bimbo all the afternoon – no doubt taking some pretty pornographic photographs - what sort of reaction am I supposed to have?'

'You're not supposed to have any sort of reaction. I happen to be a sculptor. I was a sculptor when you married me, and that's what I do. I like to sculpt the human form. I need models and I need photographs of models.'

'You used to be quite happy for me to be your model,' Rowena said, disgruntled.

Guy was not enjoying this confrontation. As calmly as he could, he said, 'Oh Rowena, be reasonable – of course I was – but you were young then and I need young models still.'

'So I am completely rejected now I've got older – how do you think that makes me feel?'

'It shouldn't worry you at all – we've both got older. I don't reject you as my wife – but I feel that I could if you go on in this ridiculous fashion. And now I want to clear up a few things here before I lock up. Are you going home now?'

'No, I'm going to the cinema with Celia. You can get your own supper.'

Rowena flounced off and Giles sighed as he went about tying up the ends of his day.

The photographs of the beautiful Lorna came out very well. The light on her smooth body made it almost look like marble. All sorts of images of her flowed through Giles' mind and he could hardly wait to capture one in stone. He decided to sculpt her in a semi-reclining pose and he ordered his marble. When it arrived on the fork-lift truck and carefully set down in his studio he felt full of excitement and anticipation.

Meanwhile life with Rowena had become increasingly difficult. They were scarcely able to communicate with each other without Rowena rolling the conversation into an argument. Giles coped with the situation by escaping to his studio and involving himself mentally and physically into his sculpting. Slowly the figure was emerging from the stone.

'What are your plans for this latest sculpture?' Rowena enquired at breakfast one morning.

'I'd like to enter it for the Summer Exhibition.'

'But they like mostly clever modern art – not the traditional sort of thing that you do. You ought to change your style.'

'Rowena, I can't just 'change my style' – you must know that very well. I like my style, it is what I'm happy with, and no way do I wish to change it. I don't appreciate modern art – I doubt if a lot of it is art at all. When we went to Rome the beauty of the Bernini sculptures in the Villa Borghese reduced me to tears, but I could cry in horror at some of the weird things which are around today. I don't understand how so many of them are accepted for the Summer Exhibition – the art world is going mad.'

Rowena pursed her lips. 'Perhaps its you who is going mad – or is it that you wouldn't need tarty little model girls to flirt with if you didn't do 'traditional?' All you can think about is that infernal sculpture. You're obsessed with it. You don't care about me or about anything else.' She paused. 'I see she was here again the other day – your precious new model.'

'Yes, she was. And that's all she is – my model. Perhaps I am going mad, in which case I am going to the studio to happily go a bit more mad right now.' said Giles. He pushed his chair back and left the room.

Later that day Rowena drove to the studio. Giles was not there. She looked at the half-finished sculpture of the pretty girl and a feeling of uncontrollable jealousy surged through her. She had an urge to damage the figure - but then she saw the photographs.

She gathered them up and took them all away. She scrunched her suffering car out of the driveway and screeched off. As Giles returned to the studio with some newly purchased chisels he was just in time to see her car disappear around a corner.

As soon as he walked into the studio he noticed, with a gasp, that the photographs were missing. It did not take him long to realize what had happened to them. He felt hurt. He felt angry. And then something inside him snapped. 'The little bitch!' he muttered aloud.

He then carefully covered up the unfinished figure and reached for the telephone.

There was no mention of the sculpture or the photographs between Giles and Rowena during the following weeks. A strange silence had settled between them, which Giles found infinitely preferable to the discordant arguing.

Then came the time of the Summer Exhibition. Rowena did not go to the first day with Guy as she said that she was going with Celia a few days later.

'Has Giles an exhibit in this year?' enquired Celia as she and Rowena were walking along Picadilly.

'I don't know – he hasn't said.'

'I suppose he hasn't then – didn't you ask him?'

Rowena did not answer.

At the exhibition, an excited Celia squeezed through the crowd to find Rowena.

'I say,' she whispered loudly, 'there is something of Giles' – come and see!'

She led her friend in front of a clay figure.

'It's not like the things he usually does, is it?' declared Celia.

The figure was in an abstract modern idiom. It was a woman in a strange reclining pose. The face was distorted and twisted, two limbs were missing and the remaining elongated hand clutched some crumpled, unidentifiable papers.

It was entitled 'ROWENA.'

3 ~ Changing Times

'This is a silly idea,' grumbled Thelma, 'wanting to find this house you lived in goodness how many years ago. Its getting dark, its probably going to rain and you might never find it. I think that we ought to go back to the car and get to the hotel for supper.'

'I don't think that its very far now – just round this corner perhaps?' I answered, pulling my collar up, feeling the first few spots of rain. 'Over there, instead of that new-looking housing estate, was the orchard where we used to go apple scrumping.'

'This nostalgia is all very well, but I'm getting wet,' my wife responded, quickening her pace in her unsuitable shoes.

Before we rounded the next corner the familiar image of this village of my childhood unfolded in my mind – the village shop, which had been the centre of so much activity and gossip; along from that the tanners cottages, with blossom-covered walls; then the school, surrounded by its asphalt playground, where we boys had chased and scrimmaged and the girls, when not tormented by plait pulling and rope snatching by the boys, had played hopscotch and endless skipping games. I remembered the church and its adjacent well-kept churchyard where, as long as the verger was nowhere near we had played tag around the gravestones. The church faced the green, scene of many a fete, school sports days, Saturday afternoon cricket and inexpert muddy football. Near the church was the Memorial Village Hall, the venue of church concerts, sales of work in aid of good causes, the district nurse's welfare clinic and meetings of all sorts. It was a refuge for the village fete on a rainy day, and was festooned with ribbons and bows for local wedding feasts. The children's Christmas party was held there, when we had cakes and jellies and little presents from Santa – who we all knew was Mr Softly the blacksmith, hiding behind a huge white beard and a voluminous red garment.

The road straightened out – and there it all was – at first glance looking very much the same.

'I suddenly feel 8 years old again!' I said whimsically to Thelma, who was smiling indulgently through the trickles of rain which were running off her hair and down her face.

'I see what you mean Jeff,' she said, 'it's charming! Where's your old house?'

'Off a little lane on the other side of the green,' I answered, '– we'll walk right round – I think the rain is stopping a bit now.'

The first thing we passed was the village shop – except that it was no longer the village shop, but now a rather tatty-looking Chinese Takeaway. It was closed, and some joker had stuck on the door an ill-written message which read- *'I thought that a dog was for life, not for lunch.'* The tanners cottages had clearly been sold (several times probably) and the row of four had been converted into two semi-detached dwellings, both very much smartened up ('if not tarted up,' Thelma said) Their once blossom-covered walls were now resplendent with hanging baskets and expensive cars stood where the front lawns had been.

Next was the school – or what had been the school. It, too had been sold. Part of it was now a private house, named 'Ye Olde School' and the other part a 'Pet's Parlour' where, the board outside declared, you could bring your pampered pets to be bathed, combed, clipped, manicured and perfumed. 'How ever,' I enquired of Thelma, 'did our farmers and shepherds manage without that facility?'

'I was wondering where the children go to school now?' Thelma said.

'I expect they are bussed to the nearest town which is about five or six miles away,' I replied, remembering straggling to and from school with my friends and coming into the cosy warmth of the central boiler in the schoolroom in the winter and playing in streams and fields on the way home on long summer afternoons.

Unchanged was the church – but the door, hitherto always open to villagers and strangers alike was now locked. against the activities of vandals and thieves. The churchyard was overgrown and in the fading light with the help of my torch, we found the graves of my grandparents and some other long-dead relations. How the village had changed since they were part of it and when it was the greater part of their world!

A lot of music and laughter, clapping and shouting was coming from the Village Hall.

Lights were flashing around the poorly curtained windows and as we drew closer we thought that there must be some sort of disco going on. Then, out from the shadows came about the last thing we would have expected – six burly policemen, complete with helmets and truncheons. A short time later there was the sound of a lot of screaming and squealing, to the accompaniment of drum rolls, rhythmic clapping and shrieks of 'Off! Off!' Take them off! Off! Off!'

Then we saw the poster on the board by the door –
COME AND SEE 'THE PEELERS'
THE FAMOUS MALE STRIPPERS.
NOT TO BE MISSED!

We stumbled, laughing, back to the road.

'Well,' said Thelma, 'I wonder what your grandparents would have thought about that? Now, where is your old house?'

'I think,' I said slowly, 'that I'll leave that memory just as it is.'

4 ~ The Paragon

'More coffee, Edward?' Pauline sat with the coffee pot poised.

'No thanks,' grunted her husband from behind the evening paper.

Pauline poured a second cup for herself and carefully replaced the elegant coffee pot on its equally elegant matching tray, where it joined the cream jug and the sugar bowl.

Neither she or Edward took sugar in their coffee these days but she always put the sugar bowl on the tray, as it completed the set. A wedding present from dear Aunt Julia, she mused, which she had enjoyed using for the last thirty eight years. It mattered a great deal to Pauline that her house was seen to be presented well, and details were important and nice things were important. A well ordered house meant to her a happy and well ordered family. Not that they had produced a large family – just the one perfect son – darling Christopher. Her eyes wandered to the side table where his handsome face smiled at her from the carefully polished silver frame. Love and pride flowed through her. He had done so well, she thought – at school and then at university and now his good job with the firm in the city. She was not sure quite what his job entailed, but she knew that it was something important – and well paid, judging by the presents he gave them – such a dear generous boy. Edward had always been quite strict with him and she had rather indulged him and had always been very fussy about whom he had mixed with – and it had certainly all paid off – he was a great credit to them both. Her face clouded a little as she glanced at the wedding photograph half-hidden behind the other. A laughing couple, holding hands in a garden. The bride's veil gently tossed by a breeze, revealing a very pretty, happy face. She certainly had good reason to look very pleased with herself, thought Pauline – she had done well trapping Christopher. She was not, of course, good enough for him. Not so well educated, although she seemed to be doing well at her management job – just had a promotion she had been told. 'Oh yes, Christopher's wife has a nice little job,' she was telling her next-door neighbour only the other day. She did not, however, think that Alison was sufficiently particular about her house or that she looked after Christopher as well as he deserved. And there was no talk of a family. Didn't she want any babies? Christopher would make a wonderful father.

'What's on the box tonight?' Edward's voice broke into her reverie.

'I don't think anything very interesting,' Pauline answered, handing him the Radio Times, 'there never seems to be these days.'

'Might be some football,' said Edward, reaching for the remote control and pressing the buttons in turn. As the screen turned green and shouting and cheering came from the television corner Pauline picked up the coffee tray and took it into the kitchen.

As she was polishing the coffee pot dry the telephone shrilled. 'I'll get it!' she shouted to Edward, as even if he had heard it she knew he would not like to be disturbed away from the football.

'Hello?'

'It's Alison,' said the answering voice.

'Oh, Alison – there's a surprise!'

'I wondered if I could come and see you?'

'Of course, when would you like to come – and naturally Christopher as well?'

'No, just me, and could I come this evening?'

'This evening? Is everything all right? You sound a bit strange.'

'I'll see you in about half an hour.'

'Alison! Alison!' But the phone had reverted to the dialling tone.

Pauline rushed into the sitting room. Her heart was pounding and her words tumbled out in panic. 'Edward! Edward! That was Alison on the phone. She is coming round – by *herself*. She sounded odd. I think something awful must have happened to Christopher! Oh please nothing awful has happened to Christopher! Alison put the phone down before I could ask her any more.'

'Calm down, there's probably quite a simple explanation. When is she coming?'

'She must be leaving straight away – she said she would be here in about half an hour. She never comes here by herself!'

'That's true – probably because you don't make her feel very welcome.'

'Well, you never seem to have much to say to her,' Pauline said accusingly, 'all you want to do when they are here is talk to Christopher.'

Edward shrugged and ran his fingers through his thinning hair. 'I'll give Christopher a ring on his mobile.'

But the automated voice at the end of the mobile informed Edward that no one was available to speak to him at the moment and would he like to leave a message.

He put the phone down crossly and all they could do was wait.

Impatiently they waited, until there was a ring at the door and they both rushed to open it.

Alison stood under the shining porch light. One side of her face was red and blue and swollen and her eye almost closed. Her fair hair was streaked with blood.

'I knew there was something wrong!' shrieked Pauline 'You've had an accident! Where's Christopher – is he hurt? Is he in hospital?'

Edward interrupted, putting his arm gently around Alison, 'Let the Alison in, Pauline, for goodness sake, and give her a chance to tell us about it.'

Alison allowed herself to be led into the sitting room and helped into an armchair.

She looked at the anxious faces staring at her. In a quiet, sad voice she said, 'This is a very hard thing for me to say, and a hard thing for you to hear. There has been no accident – your son did this to me quite, quite deliberately.'

28

'I simply do NOT believe that!' said Pauline, outraged and vehement.

'Not Christopher! Not our boy!' Edward had gone pale.

Alison looked at them in sympathy, knowing what hurt she was imparting. 'Whether you believe it or not – and I can quite understand how you don't want to – it is true, and it has been going on for some time. But this time it was more violent than before. I have put up with his gambling and with his affairs – but I am not going to give him the chance to do this sort of thing any more. This time I am leaving him, and I thought I would come and tell you.'

There was silence. Pauline was screaming inside – but could make no sound. She waited for Edward to say something, but he was just standing, stunned, looking aghast at Alison, who rose painfully to her feet. Tears ran down the mess that was her face. 'I'm so sorry,' she almost whispered, 'I know what a pedestal Christopher was on for you and I know that you were not happy about him marrying me – but I loved him too – I still do in a way – and I thought it would all work out all right. I'm sure that none of us thought that it would end like this.' She dabbed at a trickle of blood which had started to ooze from her temple. 'I must go now – I feel a bit wobbly. My parents are waiting for me. They are taking me to the hospital and then I am going back home with them.'

Unbelievably, unimaginably, the stricken Pauline and Edward knew that this nightmare was the truth. In those seconds Pauline's head was filled with so many scrambling and conflicting emotions that she felt dizzy and almost detached. Then she put her arm around Alison as they went to the front door. Before opening it and without speaking, Pauline gave Alison a soft kiss on her undamaged cheek, as if to ask her forgiveness. Forgiveness for her son and for her, too. She then went back into the sitting room.

Edward was slumped in his armchair, in a state of shock At that moment Pauline felt closer to him than she had in a long time. This pain they must bear together and help support their poor daughter-in-law and somehow help their damaged son. She knew that she would always love him, but she did not, just at present, want to see his face smiling at her so confidently. She reached for the photograph and gently but firmly turned it face down.

5 ~ Mr Jericho Jones

Jericho Jones was slumped in his electronic reclining chair. He jabbed at a button to recline it further and the chair almost jerked him out backwards. This rush of activity intensely annoyed Montezuma the tabby cat, who, asleep on Jericho's lap was not expecting to be disturbed in such a fashion and leapt off it with a sharp yowl.

Jericho swore at the chair and manoeuvred it into another position. Then he swore at the cat which was glowering at him from the synthetic rug which had pretentions of being a zebra.

Twice married, twice divorced and childless, Jericho was retired on a comfortable pension. For the best part of the last year he had been very involved in the design and construction of his new house and then in its furnishings, fittings and the installation of a great deal of the latest technology. The architects, the builders, the plumbers, the carpenters, the electricians, the roofers, the glaziers, the interior designers and the various other craftsmen and labourers who had been involved with the house had all been plagued by Mr Jericho Perfectionist Jones, who had queried and inspected every detail.

He looked around now at his large living room, with its designer furniture, designer lighting, bare floors (apart from the two zebra-like rugs) and its shining chrome and black leather. It was the last word in minimalism – very functional and very male – and now, he decided, really rather boring. A huge television screen dominated one wall and there was a console of electronics which at the touch of a button or two could bring all sorts of visual and audio wonders into the room. He was not, however in the mood for anything which was on offer. His last wife he mused, would hate this house. She had gone off with an impecunious potter and they live, it seems quite happily, in a small country cottage with chintz curtains and roses round the door.

Most of his garden was covered in paving and gravel in the interest of low maintenance. He knew nothing about plants and flowers as his wives had been involved with those, and in any case he had no desire to be fluffed around with pots and hanging baskets, so he was hardly going to find himself a slave to the garden. His golf handicap was fairly acceptable but he had let his membership of the golf club lapse and had not felt motivated to renew it. His interest in other sports was limited to occasionally watching them on television. During his working years he had no time or inclination to take up hobbies or to join local clubs, and since he had moved to the outskirts of this small town he had made no effort to interest himself in what might be going on, because by no stretch of his imagination did he consider himself a social person – in fact he found most people rather bothersome.

However, now his house was completed and running like an efficient machine. it felt strangely empty and quiet. But wasn't this what he was waiting for – time and peace to do what he wanted to do when he wanted to do it? But what did he want to do? He had little idea. He was completely and utterly bored He felt that he wanted to do something different, something even rash – anything to jolt him out of his boredom.

Mrs Pearson, his newly appointed daily housekeeper, had left him a ham salad for supper, neatly covered in cling film. He didn't fancy ham salad for supper – he would go and eat out instead.

'I'm going out, Montezuma!' he announced to the cat, who took little notice, 'and I don't know what time I'll be back.' Soon there was the impressive noise which his Aston Martin made as it backed out of the garage and glided down the drive.

A short time later he was striding along the High Street with his coat collar up against the cold of the winter evening. Darkness was already falling and the streets and shops were all brightly lit. He passed the hardware shop and the greengrocers, the bicycle and sports shop and the newsagents. Next to the newsagents was a jewellers, quietly shining. On a sudden whim, he went inside. He looked around idly as the shopkeeper was busy showing a couple some item or other about which they could not make up their minds. Leaving them busy pondering, the shopkeeper went into the back of the shop to bring something else to show them. During that very short time an extraordinary and inexplicable impulse came over Jericho and he reached into the window, removed a small tray of signet rings and very quickly slipped out of the shop.

The indecisive couple did not notice him and the returning shopkeeper was quite unaware of what had happened. Jericho continued to stride down the High Street. He could hardly believe what he had done or what motivated him to do it! At first he experienced a strange thrill, but then he felt that everyone must be looking at him suspiciously, – but then he thought that they weren't. Who would suspect such a well-dressed respectable and prosperous-looking man to be a common thief? In the fading light he made for the nearby park and sat on an available empty bench seat. He surreptitiously removed the rings from the velvet covered tray and put them in his coat pocket. He then slipped the tray into the open mouth of a nearby litter bin.

Now what was he going to do? He had had the excitement of commiting a theft undetected, but now he must get rid of the evidence!

The park was almost deserted now and walking on a little further he saw a poor, thin ragged old lady on a bench. She appeared to be asleep and had an old felt hat pulled down over her face. A bored-looking dog was lying at her feet. The dog, at least, thought Jericho, looked quite well-nourished. There was an empty bowl nearby and also a plastic container of water. Together with a collection of coins which happened to be in his pocket, Jericho threw the rings into the bowl and hurried on. He walked back to the car park, got into his car and unhurriedly drove home.

'Well!' he exclaimed to Montezuma who was rubbing himself around his legs because he decided he was hungry and suffering neglect, 'I've done something different tonight, for sure – its given me quite a lift! Can't imagine what came over me – must have had some sudden rush of blood to my head! I'll celebrate by giving you some salmon for supper – but I better eat Mrs Pearson's ham salad as I forgot I was going to eat out instead.'

In a euphoric mood he ceremoniously gave Montezuma his salmon and sat down at the kitchen table to his less exotic ham salad.

His euphoria, however, did not last for long The following evening Jericho and Montezuma were, once more, ensconced in the electronic reclining armchair. Montezuma was all right – purring contentedly but his master was reflecting gloomily about his illogical, pointless and foolhardy actions of the previous evening. What aftermath could he expect? All he had achieved, after the initial surge of excitement he had experienced was to add apprehension to his sense of uselessness and boredom.

What if he had been caught on a CCTV camera? If that old lady tried to sell the rings they may be traced back to the shop. What then? The police would be involved. He might even end up in prison!

Then the doorbell rang. His heart went into his mouth. He was expecting no one and he certainly wanted to see no one. He decided not to answer. Then the bell went again, and again and he felt compelled to respond. He dumped Montezuma unceremoniously on the floor – much, of course, to his displeasure and he put on his usual glowering expression and twitched his tail crossly.

'All right! All right!' Jericho grumbled loudly as the bell sounded once more and he was fumbling with his complicated security system. With relief he could see, through the frosted glass panel of the front door that he was not going to be confronted by a couple of burly policemen. He eventually half opened the door, ready to say something dismissive - but there, to his surprise stood a slender, very attractive smiling girl. Behind her, in the drive, stood a red somewhat battered mini.

'Yes?' he almost barked, as no other response came into his head.

The girl reached into a Sainsbury's eco-friendly jute bag and produced a small bank cash bag inside of which something gold was glistening.

'I'm sorry to disturb you,' she said politely, 'but I think that you dropped these by mistake last night.'

To say that Jericho was dumfounded was an understatement. His eyes widened and his mouth dropped open, as he realised what the bag contained. However, he quickly pulled himself together and cleared his throat. 'Perhaps you would like to come in?' he asked the girl, in rather a small voice as he opened the door wider.

'Thank you,' she said, stepping into the hall.

Jericho led her into the sitting room and motioned her to a chair. She was really lovely, he thought. She was wearing the statutory jeans and over-large sweater and her rich dark chestnut hair was gathered back loosely with some sort of fastening. Escaping strands fell very attractively around her face. Who, he wondered, was going to come up with an explanation – and what explanation could he have? He was feeling at a distinct disadvantage. Jericho Jones was not used to feeling at a disadvantage, and he wasn't very good at it. However, the girl came to the rescue.

'You see,' she began to explain, 'I spent last night on the street.'

'Good God!' Jericho burst out, 'whatever for!?'

'I work for a charity called 'Help the Homeless' and the workers and volunteers had a sponsored sleep out last night – partly to raise money and partly to find out what it is really like having to sleep on the streets – or in my case in the park.'

'Good God!' he said again.

'I was sitting on the seat not far from the car park,' the girl went on, 'and you came striding along and dropped these into Percy's bowl.' She proffered the little bag of rings.

'Who's Percy?' Jericho asked as he reached to take the bag.

'My dog of course – he lives at home with my parents most of the time and he didn't think much of a night out in the great outdoors – he looked very dejected. But he was company and he would have protected me and would never have left me. I can quite understand why homeless people often have dogs – they are so unjudgemental'.

So this delightful creature was masquerading as the pathetic skinny woman with a hat pulled down over her face whom he had encountered last night! What now? Jericho felt surprise, relief, amusement and a a silly fool all at once. He left the ball very much in her court as she continued.

'When I saw that what was in the bowl was obviously valuable and you must have made a mistake, I tried to run after you, but I had such strange large shoes on which someone had given me to wear that I couldn't run properly and you had reached your car (what a car by the way!) and were about to drive off.'

'So then what did you do?'

'My little old car was fortunately fairly near and I had my keys with me, so Percy and I leapt into it and managed to follow you, hoping that you were local. Fortunately you were not being a speed merchant and I managed to keep behind you. But when you turned into this drive leading to such a posh house, I felt that I couldn't arrive on your doorstep as a down-and-out and that I would come back when I was looking a bit more respectable. So here I am.'

'So you are.' Jericho said appreciatively, 'it is very good of you to come back with the rings – I am very grateful to you.' He wondered whatever she would think if she knew she was handling stolen goods! She asked for no explanation and he gave none. 'What is your name?'

'Charlotte – but people call me Charlie. What's yours?'

'Jericho Jones.'

She looked at him with her clear blue-green eyes open wide. A smile began to play around her mouth. 'You're joking?' she said.

'No I'm not.'

'You mean that your name really is Jericho Jones?'

'Yes, it really is.'

'Would you mind very much if I laughed a little bit?'

'Not in the least,' he found himself saying, 'laugh as much as you like.'

So she did – giggles which developed into full blown laughter, which he found so utterly delightful and infectious that he joined in because he couldn't help himself. He laughed like he hadn't laughed in a long time. After the hilarity had died down he asked her if she would like a drink.

'I'd love a mug of coffee,' she replied.

'My housekeeper isn't here, but I think I can manage that,' he said.

'I'll come and help you,' and she followed him out into the kitchen, which looked like a stainless steel laboratory.

'Does your housekeeper look after you nicely/'

'Oh yes, fairly nicely.'

'That's good,' she said.

The coffee made, they were back in the sitting room. Charlie cupped her hands around her mug and let Montezuma jump on her lap. He was wide-eyed and all dramatic because he could smell Percy all over her jeans.

'Tell me what you do about these wretched people who are homeless.' said Jericho.

'They are not wretched *people* – but they are wretched because they're homeless.'

'Why can't they pull themselves together and get themselves a job and some digs?'

'It's not as easy as that, and many of them are not very employable, for a variety of reasons.'

'Then doesn't this Welfare State of ours shower them with benefits?'

'No, not if they are 'of no fixed abode.'

'I see – so what does your charity do about it?'

'We run a Soup Kitchen and a Night Shelter and by a great stint of fund-raising and some generous grants we have managed to buy a couple of properties and create bed-sitting rooms in them. People have been generous about giving furniture etc. So we've successfully housed several people like that and then they can hopefully get a job, or start receiving housing benefit and can pay us rent, which goes towards the fairly small mortgages we negotiated. But there are *so* many rules and regulations to cope with you wouldn't *believe*.'

'Oh, I think I would', said Jericho. Charlie intrigued him and he wanted to know more about her. 'How did you get involved in all this to start with?' he asked.

She smiled and wrinkled up her nose. 'Well, when I left university I was going to study law, but have a 'year out' first – as one does – but it seemed to me that there were enough 'year outers' traipsing around Ayers Rock or trying to save Africa and so I thought I'd try and do something here instead, hopefully a little bit helpful. I've certainly learnt a lot doing it, in all sorts of ways. My parents, I think, are just a bit worried that I'll want to do it for a bit too long!' She gazed around his state of the modern world room.

'Are you retired?' she asked.

'Yes.'

'Let me guess – are you an – um –architect?'

'No, I trained as an accountant and then got involved in various business ventures.'

'Oh, I see,' she said, then, 'I'm sorry – I didn't mean to pry.'

'I don't mind,' he said truthfully.

They sat chatting for quite a while longer. This girl was like a breath of fresh air to Jericho – she was captivating, she was enthusiastic – she was the daughter which he had never had. Then she said that she must go as she was on duty at the Night Shelter in a short while. She apologised to Montezuma as she lifted him from the comfort of her lap – but he appeared unforgiving. With considerable reluctance Jericho showed her out into the hall.

'Will you,' he asked, 'keep in touch? I would be interested to hear how 'Helping the Homeless' progresses.'

She sparkled a smile, 'I'd be delighted to!' she responded, and half jokingly added, 'we can always do with any help that comes our way! It has been so nice to meet you, Mr Jericho Jones – and thanks for the coffee.'

'I've enjoyed our chat', he said, 'and here is something for the return of that which I lost so carelessly.' He slipped a folded cheque into her jute bag.

'Thank you so much,' she said, having no idea how very generous the cheque was, and blowing him a kiss, she hurried off, bundled into her little car and drove away.

He watched as the car turned out into the road, noting that one of the brake lights wasn't functioning, and went back into the room. Of course it looked just the same – formal, stark, cleverly lit – but it felt as if a ray of sunshine had burst into it and it was still warm from its glow.

'Well,' he said to Montezuma, 'that was an unexpected interlude. You liked her didn't you?' Montezuma looked fairly indifferent and rubbed himself up against his master's legs. 'Well *I* liked her Montezuma'

He went over to his desk, found a strong brown envelope and firmly sealed the rings inside it. Then he went to the town and unseen, he slipped the unmarked envelope through the jewellery shop's letter box 'Thank you, Charlie,' he whispered, 'for getting me out of that!'

* * * * *

It was a month or so later, and Jericho was surprised and delighted to find Charlie on his doorstep again. 'Charlie! – Come in! Come in!' he said, and in she bounced.

'Dear Mr Jericho Jones,' she said, over her cup of coffee, 'the volunteer who has been doing our H for the H accounts is moving right down to the West Country and we badly need someone to take his place. I thought of you. I felt that I had nothing to lose by just *asking*. Could you possibly, *possibly* help us out – even if only for the time being?'

Jericho smiled. 'My dear child – of course I can. I should be pleased to.'

Mr Jericho Jones,' said the delighted Charlie, 'would you mind if I gave you a hug?'

'That would be an added bonus!' was the reply.

The hug being duly delivered, Charlie said, 'We are having a meeting next Wednesday – do you think that you could come? We have a small office over the soup kitchen, in Marsham Road. I wouldn't think it a very good idea for you to arrive in your Aston Martin. If you wouldn't mind downgrading to my old mini I could come and pick you up.' And so it was agreed.

The following Wednesday Jericho said to his housekeeper, 'You need not leave me anything for supper tonight Mrs Pearson, thank you – I'm going to a meeting – and there is a good chance that I may get a bowl of soup.'

6 ~ Goodbye

'Goodbye!' she said, zipping up her bag. 'I'm going.'

'I can see that,' he said, peering at her round his newspaper, ' – you've got your coat on.'

'I'm leaving.'

'Yes, when'll you be back?'

'I'm not coming back.'

'What d'you mean?'

'I'm leaving you – I'm walking out of your life.'

'Don't be silly. Where you going?'

'I'm not quite sure.'

'Well, are you going on a bus or a train, or are you getting a taxi?'

'I thought I'd take the car.'

'Don't forget that getting her in and out of third gear's a bit dicey – needs double de-clutching.'

'I can't do that very well.'

'Make sure you push the clutch right home then. Don't be too late back tonight.'

'I told you – I'm not coming back.'

'Tomorrow then.'

'But I'M LEAVING YOU. I'm not coming back – why can't you take me seriously? One of the reasons that I'm leaving you is that you don't take me seriously.'

'Yes I do.'

'No you don't – you just take me for granted.'

'How am I going to get to work in the morning if you've got the car?'

'You'll have to get a No.27 bus.'

'The No.27 doesn't stop outside the factory – it goes the other way round.'

'No. 14 then.'

'Mm – No.14 would probably be all right.'

'They're not very frequent though – make sure you wrap up warm or you might get a bad cold waiting at the bus stop. Your nice thick scarf is in the drawer in the hall.'

'OK.'

'Are you going to make yourself some sandwiches for lunch tomorrow or have something in the canteen?'

'I don't know yet. What is there to put in the sandwiches?'

'There's plenty of cheese in the frig.'

'What about Branston pickle? I can't have cheese sandwiches without Branston pickle.'

'It's in the left-hand cupboard, middle shelf. There's a good half jar.'

'And have I got a clean shirt?'

'All your shirts and T shirts are clean and hanging up in your cupboard – and when you've run out of clean ones you'll have to do some washing.'

'What, in the washing machine? How do I work it?'

'Come along and I'll show you – but hurry up, I wanted to be off by now – you're holding me up.'

'As we're in the kitchen we might just as well have a cup of tea – I'll put the kettle on.'

'All right then. Now – you put the washing in – don't mix the white things with your socks, as that will make the white things a bad colour, and don't squash too many things in or they won't get washed properly. You put the washing powder – this packet here – in this side of the drawer, close it, set the programme and press this red button to start.'

'How do I know what programme to set?'

'1 for soaking, 2 for hot, 3 for coloured things, 5 for woollen things – oh – you'll just have to read the instructions, I'll leave them here, on the top of the machine.'

'The kettle's boiling now, shall I make the tea?'

'That'll be nice.'

'Where's the tea?'

'In the caddy in front of you, where its always been.'

'How much shall I put in?'

'Two bags.'

'There we are then. How much water?'

'Half fill the pot. I'll just drink mine and then I'll be off.'

'Are you sure you want to go?'

'Yes.'

'And leave me?'

'Yes.'

'Why?'

'I told you – I'm fed up with being taken for granted. I'm not going to stay here and let you walk over me as if I'm a doormat any longer.'

'I don't walk over you as if you are a doormat.'

'Yes you do – at least that's what it feels like to me.'

'Oh – really? Anyway, how am I going to manage without you?'

'Judging by this cup of tea – not very well. Are you sure the water was boiling?'

'I thought it was. And anyway, what are you going to do when you leave me, not to come back. Where are you going to go?'

'I'll probably go to mother's to start with.'

'Then what? She hasn't got enough room for you to stay for long, and anyway you argue all the time with your sister and you don't like the dog because it smells.'

'I know, – but I'll think of something.'

'What?'

'I don't know yet, do I?'

'Well, I don't think that you ought to go.'

'Oh, why not?'

'Because you don't seem to have thought it through properly. You ought to have some sort of *plan*,'

'Yes, I suppose I ought.'

'Anyway, you need me to look after you.'

'I need *you* to look after *me* – you're the one who gets looked after all the time!'

'But I go out to work and pay the mortgage – and I put those shelves up in the kitchen last year.'

'True – they have fallen down now – but you did put them up.'

'I think that you take me for granted – like you say I take you for granted.'

'Perhaps you're right. But I'm still going to go.'

'Well, I'm not at all keen on the idea. Anyway – I'd – well, I'd miss you.'

'Would you?'

'Yes, I would, I'd miss you.'

'Why? Because you don't want to wash your own shirts or make your own sandwiches or cook your own supper?'

'Well, that as well.'

'As well as what?'

'As because – because – I love you. And I don't want you to go.'

'Well – its taken you a long time to say that. I'll take my coat off then, and this time I'd better make the tea.'

7 ~ Modern Art

Elizabeth was waiting for me at the corner table in the café as we had arranged. Slightly to my surprise she had someone with her.

'Linda dear,' Elizabeth greeted me warmly, 'lovely to see you! I knew that you wouldn't mind if my friend Cecelia joined us today – she's staying with me for a couple of days.'

'Of course not. Nice to meet you, Cecelia.'

Cecelia beamed from under a woolly hat which resembled a tea cosy, underneath which small bunches of frizzy hair escaped.

'Delighted! Delighted!' she enthused.

Over our cappuccinos we discussed plans for the day – shopping for an outfit for Elizabeth and then a matinee.

'Could I make one plea for the day?' Cecelia asked eagerly, 'I see there is a modern art exhibition in the hall which we passed. I just adore art, especially modern art – its just *me*, somehow. I'm a bit of a connoisseur, you know.'

Elizabeth and I said we were both quite happy to view the modern art, although, as it so happened, neither of us had much interest or knowledge about it.

When we arrived at the hall Cecelia rushed into the first room by the entrance and gazed around short-sightedly making little squeals of delight. She then fumbled a pair of large-rimmed glasses out of her tapestry bag and donned them, which gave her a distinctly owl-like appearance. All around the room was displayed a somewhat strange collection of paintings. The first one consisted of six or seven white blobs on a green background.

Cecelia stood in front of it quite entranced.

'Charming, charming!' she exclaimed, 'and yet also so exciting and dramatic – the white simply bursts out of the green, don't you think – so very clever – so significant!'

Significant of quite what Elizabeth and I were left to surmise and came to no conclusion.

Cecelia wafted on to the next picture, her long skirt swaying dramatically as she moved.

'This one is more after the Dhali school I feel,' she said, 'a little sinister, don't you think- with the head not quite attached to the body and one arm missing – his human cannibal phase.'

The next picture consisted of a large blob of lightness in the centre of a sea of brown.

Cecelia decided that it amazingly depicted something in outer space. And then she became very animated about another – a strange spider-like figure with swirls of green around it.

'Lovely, lovely!' she breathed, so very similar to a painting which was in the Summer Exhibition last year – Woman and Watercress it was called – so full of, well full of *meaning*.'

And so Cecelia glided around the room, admiring, criticizing, commenting knowingly, with Elizabeth and I trailing behind feeling half amused and half bewildered.

I stared at one painting that was just one mass of crazy swirling colours. I couldn't believe my eyes as the colours came and went seeming to engulf me. What it was supposed to represent I could not imagine, but I was not moved to ask Cecelia's opinion, as she was completely absorbed in a painting on the other side of the room, stepping away from it and then nearer again, making strange squeaking noises in her excitement.

The painting consisted of rather wobbly circles and short lines, some in orange and some in purple.

'A circle in a spiral like a wheel within a wheel.' Cecelia murmured. 'Isn't that an example of such artistic talent? I wonder who the artist is? I can't understand this squiggle in the corner – and we haven't a catalogue – we must have a catalogue!'

Elizabeth and I said we'd go in search of one and went out into the corridor where we found a lady seated at a table engrossed in her knitting.

'Would it be possible to have a catalogue of the paintings in the exhibition please?' I asked.

'Of course! They're on the table as you go in. Go through the swing door just on the right there.' She waved a knitting needle in the appropriate direction.

'Will that include the paintings in the room we have just left?'

'Bless you no, – that's the room where the nursery school is held three days a week. – the children love to have their pictures put up on the walls.'

She looked at us in alarm as we threatened to injure ourselves laughing.

But it wasn't going to be so funny telling Cecelia.

8 ~ The Hat

'*A*nd the beautiful princess married the handsome prince and they lived happily ever after.' Tom closed the book and grinned at his small niece, whose shining eyes peeped at him over her duvet.

'Uncle Tom, the princes and princesses always marry each other in the stories, don't they?'

'Mmm, they do.'

'But do they always *really*, if they're not in a story?'

Tom laughed and ruffled her still bath-damp hair. 'No, not always.'

'I wish I could meet a beautiful princess.' She was back in her fairytale again.

'You go off to sleep now, and you may dream about one.'

He bent down to kiss her and two arms sprang from the covers and clasped him tightly round his neck. 'I love you, big Uncle Tom. You are going to come to my party aren't you? It's *soon*, and I'm going to be *six*.'

'Lovely – I'll be there! Goodnight now.'

'Night,' and sleepily, 'I hope I do dream about a princess.'

In the kitchen Tom's sister gave him a beer. 'What are you doing next weekend? It's Emma's party on Sunday. I'm sure that a host of six year-olds having a party isn't quite your favourite scene – but she would be very disappointed if you didn't come.'

'I know – I've just been reminded – but despite what you say I really wouldn't like to miss it. I'm going to that wedding the day before – second cousin what's- his- name.'

'Oh, of course, I forgot – we had to refuse – its too far – and they didn't want the children'

'And,' Tom added, 'the parentals will be on holiday – so Mother twisted my arm to go. 'Someone must represent our branch of the family, dear.' *And* its in the depths of Suffolk, *and* I should be playing in a rugger match. I hardly know cousin thingy – I don't think I've seen him since we had a fight over a model aeroplane when we were about twelve. I won the fight, but he broke the aeroplane. I won't know a soul at the wedding.'

'Poor Tom!' his sister said, giving him another beer and an affectionate hug, 'what a trying weekend you're in for!'

* * * * *

The following Saturday Tom edged his large frame into a pew in a spacious East Anglian church. A subdued mutter of voices from the gathered and gathering congregation merged with the soft playing of the organ. Fingering his 'Order of Service' and thinking wistfully about the rugger match, he gazed idly around at the wedding guests, the church officials and the fidgeting choir boys.

Then the hat caught his eye. It was settled three or four pews in front of him. Deliciously feminine, it had a wide brim of pale straw in which a large white silk flower nestled, and draped around the whole was some gossamer material which somehow or other ended up around the wearer's shoulders. It was an enchanting hat and it bobbed gently as the girl underneath it chatted to her man.

Tom stared up at the vaulted ceiling, at the flowers, at the nervous bridegroom sitting next to his best man in the front pew. But his eyes kept wandering back to the hat.

What did the girl who was wearing it look like? He could not see her face. He was conscious of vaguely envying the man sitting next to the hat, and hoped that he appreciated it

There was a flurry of activity at the back of the church, heralding the arrival of the bride.

The congregation ceased its muted conversations and rose untidily to its feet as the organ started to play the Bridal March. All eyes turned towards the aisle to glimpse the bride. All eyes except Tom's. Here was his chance to see the face underneath the hat. The hat turned. Its wearer was smiling. Tom caught his breath and clutched the back of the pew in front. He felt hot. Then cold. His mouth went dry and his heart thumped wildly inside his best suit. It was Imogen! The wearer of the hat was Imogen! It was just the sort of hat she would wear. Imogen – who had broken his heart seven years and eight and a half months ago.

'*Dearly beloved, we are gathered together*,' the vicar began. He could have been reciting 'Mary had a Little Lamb' for all Tom was aware. He was sitting on a seat on London's South Bank and all he could hear was his last conversation with Imogen. It was a warm soft late summer evening and London and the Thames looked wonderful. Tom would have dived into the Thames for Imogen. He would have climbed up Nelson's column for Imogen. He was bursting with a first passionate love for her and he wanted to be with her for ever. He tried to tell her so.

'Hush, dear Tom,' she had breathed, gently touching his mouth with her fingers, 'we are not ready for any sort of commitment – we have lots to do – probably in different directions – and neither of us really know quite which direction to go in.'

'All I know is that I want to go in your direction – wherever it is going.' Tom had said desperately.

She had smiled her lovely smile. 'You would probably decide that it was not the right way at all. We've had a lovely time together – I'll never forget it – don't let's spoil it by letting it get stale and mundane. And thank you.' She had cupped his face in her hands, kissed him and said, 'I'm going now Tom – please don't try and stop me – its best.'

'*For better, for worse, for richer for poorer*'---- but Tom was still sitting on the Embankment watching Imogen disappear in a haze of blue dress and fair hair, as the lights along the river misted into each other.

He knew better than to persue her – then or at any time. He lost touch with friends they had in common. He didn't want to be told by anyone else what she was doing, where she was living, who she was with, if she was married. Not that he never wondered – but he didn't have to know, and it was all so painful.

He sat down hurriedly as he realised that he was the only member of the congregation left standing. His eyes kept returning to the hat. He remembered the hurt and the dark days. London without Imogen, weekends without Imogen – life without Imogen

'*Love Divine, all loves excelling.*' Everyone was on their feet again. The hat was swaying gently to the rhythm of the hymn.

Gradually he had felt that the wound had started to heal and the darkness to lift. There were other girls of course, but never another like Imogen. He never really thought that there would be. He was making a success of his career, was still a powerful asset to the rugger team and had a good social life – but however much he tried he could never put Imogen right out of his mind. And now, after all this time – here she was, underneath this wonderful hat, sitting with her man – lucky devil.

The wedding service continued more or less without Tom, apart from the space he was taking up in the pew, and shortly the bridal party was making its way to the vestry to sign the register. A mezzo soprano began to sing 'Ave Maria.'

Tom stared fixedly at the hat. How was he going to play this one? A small part of him wanted to simply disappear – but he knew he wouldn't do that. He could approach the couple in an aura of bonhomie. 'My goodness what a surprise! Ha! ha! However are you? Ha! ha!' Kiss Imogen, pump husband's hand and say how absolutely marvellous everything is etc. But that wouldn't do – it wasn't quite his style and he'd make a fool of himself. He felt he was going to make a fool of himself whatever he did.

The mezzo soprano reached her last note. Tom sat unmoving. His feet were lead.

The dramatic opening chords of The Wedding March filled the church and the bride and bridegroom led the procession down the aisle. Everyone stood, smiling, nodding and chatting whilst waiting their turn to shuffle out of the church. The hat was bobbing about excitedly. Tom managed to get to his feet. It was not until everyone had emerged from the church and gathered on the grass outside that the hat turned round. She saw him. She looked even lovelier than before. In that second, the years since they parted were as if they had never been. If he had thought that time had healed anything he was quite wrong.

'Tom! *Tom*!' She was coming towards him, arms outstretched! 'Oh Tom – what an *amazing* surprise!'

'Imogen.' It was all he could manage to say and his voice sounded as if it didn't belong to him.

She kissed him on both cheeks. The fleeting feeling of sensuous delight as her face touched his was tempered by his realisation that everyone kisses everyone else at weddings.

'I like your hat.' he said inanely.

She laughed the laugh which he remembered so well. 'Thank you Tom – but we have much more interesting things to talk about than hats! Come and meet David!'

Tom braced himself to meet the husband/ partner. He would, of course, detest him.

'David, this is Tom. Tom, my brother David.'

'Your brother – of course!' Tom just loved this man for being Imogen's brother. He shook his hand with great enthusiasm.

'Tom and I knew each other quite a few years ago,' Imogen was saying, 'I think it was when you were in Singapore, David – so I suppose you never met.'

'Probably not,' agreed David, surreptitiously rubbing his hand back to life.

'We're here because David was at college with the bridegroom. Why are you here Tom?'

'I'm some sort of cousin,' Tom answered with a vague wave of his hand.

They stood together chatting in a superficial meeting-at-a-wedding kind of way until David excused himself to greet a long lost college friend.

'Oh Tom!' said Imogen, 'We have lots of news to catch up on!' She wrinkled her nose up at him and slipped her arm easily through his. 'Doesn't the bride look lovely, by the way?'

Tom suddenly realised how very little notice he had taken of the bride. 'Yes, yes, really lovely.' he said. But he was thinking that he had to ask her – if this bubble was going to burst it was best for it to do it sooner rather than later. He turned to face her and held both her hands in his. 'Imogen,' he said, 'are you married – or anything?'

'Nope. Are you?'

'Ditto – but why aren't you?' He sounded like a schoolboy.

'I could ask you the same question! Perhaps,' she said teasingly, 'I have never met anyone else quite as nice as you? I've missed you. Tom.'

Tom could only let out some kind of groan in reply and somehow dodging her hat he kissed her – not only because everyone kisses everyone else at weddings.

The reception went by in a haze for Tom – food, drink, speeches and hubbub of voices.

Several times he thought that the sound of the voices would change into the bleep of his alarm clock and the vision of Imogen in her pale blue and pink dress and lovely hat would disappear and the dream would be over.

When the guests began to depart Tom thanked the newly weds and their parents extremely enthusiastically for inviting him to the wedding. As he hadn't seen the bridegroom or his family for years and the others never at all before, perhaps they were a little surprised – but Tom felt that this distant cousin of his was an absolutely excellent fellow and quite forgave him for breaking his aeroplane!

He then managed to extricate Imogen from a group of laughing girls.

'Imogen, are you going in my direction? Can I take you home?' Did she, he wondered, remember as well as he, their last conversation?

'She smiled up at him, 'Yes, Tom, I am going in the same direction as you. David is staying overnight with some friends, so I was going back by train. It would be lovely to come with you.'

Tom was a fairly logical chap, with a scientific training, so it was strange that as he drove through the Suffolk countryside he had the sensation that the wheels of his car were hardly touching the surface of the road.

On the back seat was the hat with the petals of its flower stirring gently in the breeze from the window.

'Imogen,' Tom said, 'are you doing anything very special tomorrow?'

'Not especially special.'

'Would you like to come to a party with me? I know someone who would very much like to meet a princess. Hats, I believe, may be worn.'

9 ~ Conversation in a Car

'Elizabeth, I won't let you do this.'

'Whatever do you mean, you won't let me do it?'

'What I say.'

'And what makes you think you have suddenly any right to tell me what I can and what I can't do?'

'Well, I am your husband.'

'Yes, I'm aware of that – but we never said the obey thing – ours is supposed to be the sort of marriage with both of us being free spirits. What's got into you all of a sudden?'

'Nothing's got into me – I just don't want you to do this – no husband would.'

'Absolute rubbish. I've said I'll do it and I shall. Anyway, where is your sense of community service?'

'I don't see where community service comes into it.'

'Well I do.'

'How?'

'Well, – it just does.'

'Nonsense!'

'Well, I think it's a useful thing to do – and mind that chap on his bike!'

'You needn't tell me how to drive the car.'

'Drive it properly then.'

'Now whose dictating to who?'

'To *whom*.'

'My grammar is immaterial to the subject in hand.'

'True – but I don't wish to discuss the subject any further – I'm going next Monday and that's that.'

'But you know perfectly *well* that I don't want you to go.'

'Yes, you've made that very clear and I think that you're being stupid and unreasonable.'

'How many people in the group?'

'Not sure. Ten or twelve perhaps?'

'I think its disgusting.'

'What's disgusting about it for goodness sake – they've got to learn.'

'Well they needn't learn on you.'

'They've got to practice on someone.'

'What if you know some of them – that'll be embarrassing?'

'No it won't.'

'Anyway, you'll get cold.'

'No I won't – its quite warm in there.'

'What if the heating system breaks down?'

'Then we'll all get cold – but don't be silly its not likely to break down, although I expect you'd like it to.'

'No I wouldn't – you might get pneumonia.'

'Then you could say I told you so.'

'You won't be able to talk either – you won't like that.'

'True – but I'll manage. I'll pretend that I'm dead.'

'You'll have to keep very still – you're not very good at that either.'

'I know, but I'll be in the water some of the time.'

'In the water!? Like Venus rising from the sea? What water? How much water?'

'In a swimming pool, Gerald dear, there is usually quite a lot of water.'

'Whatever has the swimming pool got to do with it? What's the art class doing at the swimming pool?'

'The art class? It's got nothing to do with the art class. Mind that car – its turning right.

'Whatever are you talking about – or are you just going soft in the head?'

'You said that you were going to be a model for the life class.'

'No I didn't – I said I was going to be a model for the life SAVING class – their plastic one refused to be resuscitated.'

'Oh, that's all right then – sorry, I misunderstood.'

'Gerald, it is not all right. I've discovered that you can be dictatorial, chauvinistic and a prude. What about our free spirits? I am revising my view of our marriage.'

'Don't be so ridiculous.'

'There you go again. At least the art class which you seem to have such an objection to wouldn't be 'hands on' but I expect the would-be life savers will all be queuing up to give me mouth to mouth resuscitation – one by one, and don't you dare say that I'm not to go on Monday, because I expect in the long run I shall help save lots of people from drowning. That's what I mean by community spirit – and look out – you're going to scrape the car on the wall as you drive in!'

10 ~ Seeing The Funny Side

Steve wandered disconsolately round the market, slowly swinging a green plastic bag backwards and forwards as he went. It contained some tomatoes, a bargain pack of three pairs of socks, a bargain pack of Double A batteries and a lump of cheddar cheese. He felt at a loose end, and the market was just somewhere to go.

'Cuppla melons for a pound Guv?' shouted the man behind a mound of apples and oranges, as Steve drifted past his stall, waving a disinterested hand.

'Luverly ripe mangoes – half the shop prices!' another vendor was yelling.

What, Steve wondered, would he want with a mango? He didn't think that he had ever had a mango in his life – and today wasn't the day to start doing anything different, even eating a mango – he just didn't have the motivation. He had no plans for the rest of the day. A number of his mates had gone off in a coach, in a blaze of blue and white, to cheer Portsmouth playing Wolverhampton Wanderers. He wasn't on the coach because he had promised Linda that he would go with her to a family party. One of her aunts was supposed to be rejoicing in the fact that she had reached her three score years and ten.

Steve didn't think that that was much to rejoice about, but said he would go and join in the rejoicing – if there was any. And then he and Linda had started arguing. He couldn't rightly remember what it was all about, but didn't think that it had anything to do with the aunt and the party. However, it ended with Linda stomping out and banging the flat door very loudly in her going and he hadn't heard from her since. Now he dearly wished that he had gone on that coach to Wolverhampton. Not that he and Linda had had a really passionate affair, but they had an uncomplicated fun time together and this Saturday he was finding her absence a distinct gap.

He idled about the market for a bit longer, bought a pork pie and a second-hand *Star Wars* video and had just decided to go off and have a beer when he saw the girl. She was quite a few stalls away from him, studying some lipsticks. Without doubt she was the most beautiful of creatures. She was tall and elegant and had the most wonderful head of blonde hair that Steve thought he had ever seen. It curled gently to her shoulders, falling softly around her face as she bent to look at the wares on the stall.

Steve watched her until she made a purchase and turned away from the stall. From a distance he kept his eyes on her as she went round the market. Her amazing blonde hair was so easy to see and almost without realizing it he found himself walking about discreetly so that he kept her in view. Why? Well, for one thing he had nothing else to do and he was always very attracted to blonde girls – but they were nearly always engrossed with some fortunate and not unattractive male – but here was this amazing eyeful unaccompanied and not looking as if she was hell bent on engrossing herself in anything particularly immediate. Now she was leaving the market and Steve couldn't stop himself from following her. It was worth a chance! As he walked behind her watching her swaying hair, he fantasized about running his fingers through it, burying his face in it and moving it aside to whisper sweet nonsense in an ear.

She was walking quite quickly now – or as quickly as her high heeled shoes would allow. They were smart black patent shoes and she swung a matching handbag over her shoulder. She was wearing a full-skirted red dress under a black cloak and Steve thought that she looked fantastic. Feeling shabby in his worn jeans and old trainers he felt that this girl was rather too up-market for him, but nonetheless he continued to follow her at a discreet distance – his long loping strides easily keeping up with her and necessitating him every now and then to slow his pace. But how was he going to approach this goddess? What excuse or reason could he find to engage her in any sort of conversation? He thought that he probably couldn't and would probably just end up feeling a fool, so he contemplated getting to his car, driving to The Kings Arms, having a couple of beers and then going home.

They were walking behind the market now, where all the loading and unloading went on. And then it happened. His goddess somehow got one high-heeled shoe caught up with a box of cabbages which had just been unloaded from a fork lift truck – and smack! – down she went. Her handbag flew out of her hand, spewing its contents all over – and the keys in it disappeared down a large metal grating into the blackness beneath it. Gary rushed eagerly to help his beautiful maiden in distress – what a fantastic opportunity!

Then he momentarily stopped short in his tracks when he saw, on top of the cabbages, the wonderful blonde hair! The head which it had adorned was covered in close cropped dark hair and the face had a very well-shaved look.

'Good God!' Steve muttered to himself, 'she's a bloke!' However, gender aside, a helping hand was seen to be needed.

'You OK. mate?' he asked.

'Ye-es, I think so,' answered a gruff voice, 'feeling a bit of a fool!' the fallen idol added, glancing at Steve, half embarrassed, half apologetic, as he got to his feet.

'But you're not hurt, that's the main thing,' said Steve cheerfully, handing him the wig which he had retrieved from the cabbages. 'Here, you better put this back on again, you look a bit daft without it.'

'Thanks, but the worst thing is that my car keys have gone down that grating – I'll never get them from there – and the heel has come off my shoe! Oh God! What a bloody disaster!'

'Have you got a spare set of car keys at home?' Steve asked.

'Yes.'

'Well there's no great problem – you stay here – you can't walk very well with just one four inch heel. My car is just in the car park over the way – I'll bring it back here and then I'll take you home and we can collect your keys and then get your car. I hope your door key didn't go down the grating too?

'No, fortunately not. This is really very good of you. Not everyone would bother to do this for a man dressed up as a woman – they'd probably think it serves him right.'

'No problem,' reiterated Steve, 'I'm Steve, by the way. What do you call yourself?'

'Jemima when I'm in this sort of garb and Jim when I'm not.'

'I'll stick with Jim,' Steve said, as he strode off to the car park, 'won't be long!'

They were soon driving to Jim's flat. This wasn't quite how Steve had envisaged his conquest of the blonde in the red dress!

They bundled themselves into the flat and Jim ushered Steve into a comfortable living room where they each flopped into an armchair.

'I'm not gay, you know,' explained Jim – 'Just a cross dresser – I get this inexplicable urge every now and then to dress up as a woman. Otherwise I have all the other normal male urges. I have a girlfriend who is trying to decide whether she is happy to share her wardrobe with me on a permanent basis!'

'Well' said Steve, 'seems a bit weird to me – but I suppose we're all different. Personally I think it'd be a good idea to repress your girlie urges and tell your girlfriend that she can keep her wardrobe all to herself. I must say, though, I quite fancied you when I thought you were a woman – especially with all that blonde hair. I certainly don't fancy you now though – you look a nightmare!'

Jim got up and looked at himself in a long mirror in the hall. The glamorous wig was askew, he had one heeless shoe still in his hand, his face was smeared with dirt and the red dress was looking very bedraggled. The fastening at the top had become largely undone, revealing a padded bra nestling in a hairy chest. He caught Steve's eye and then they both began to laugh. They laughed and laughed until they found it difficult to stop.

'Fancy falling into a box of cabbages!' Jim spluttered, wiping his eyes.

'And to think I fancied you!' added Steve.

'You can't help seeing the funny side!' said Jim.

'Life would be pretty dull if you couldn't,' said Steve, 'I must confess that whole thing has quite cheered up my day!'

'Well, I was certainly lucky that you happened along. Can't think what would have happened if you hadn't. I might have ended up in the police station or something!'

'Hardly that', rejoined Steve, 'but things might have been a bit tricky!'

When Jim had changed into his Jeans and T shirt and washed the make-up off his face, he looked a perfectly OK. bloke's bloke. 'Let's go and have a beer at The Dog and Doublet,' he said, shrugging himself into his anorak.

'The Dog and Doublet is a straight pub, I hope?' questioned Steve.

'Straight as a dye, my friend.'

'Just checking,' grinned Steve.

11 ~ The Culprit

Gary's large bulk burst into the flat like an untidy tornado.

'Marlene!' he yelled. No answer. 'Marlene!' Even louder. 'Where the hell's this week's lottery ticket?'

Marlene emerged from the kitchen and through a haze of cigarette smoke squinted at her husband without enthusiasm.

'Dunno. Why?'

' 'Cause it may be a bloody big winner – that's why – and not just your few quid rubbish!'

This announcement almost dislodged the cigarette which was dangling from Marlene's lips.

'*May* be? What sort of may be?'

Gary waved a grubby piece of paper at her face. 'I'd written the ticket number down on here, but some beer got spilt on it and I can't see what the last number is. Its either a 5 or an 8. I was in the pub and they'd got the lottery programme on. If our last number's a 5 then I think we've won – but if its an 8 we bloody haven't.'

Marlene gaped. 'Stupid fool – why didn't you have the ticket in yer wallet?'

'For God's sake let's find it,' Gary shouted, ignoring her question.

A frantic search for the ticket then commenced – a search for the potential pot of gold.

'We can move from this 'orrible flat,' fantasised Marlene, wildly throwing settee cushions on the floor, exposing a cluster of unpleasant-looking items which had been nestling underneath them for some time. 'I've always hated it here – we'll buy a nice big house somewhere.'

Gary was churning over piles of papers and magazines like a man possessed.

'And a Porsche. And keep going on cruises. No more poxy jobs or squeezing benefits out of the Social. If you kept this place anything like tidy we wouldn't keep losing things,' he growled.

'Who d'you think you are to talk – you're a messy bastard!' Marlene retorted.

'It's your job to clean up – you only work part time in the shop round the corner. Look at the state of this place – and you keep letting the next door cat come in and spread its fleas around.'

A tabby cat was curled up on a chair in the corner of the room and the only reaction she had to the sudden whirlwind of activity going on was to flick her ears, move the tip of her tail just slightly and get back to the serious business of going to sleep.

Marlene snorted her contempt at Gary. 'Chauvinist pig!' she spat, 'anyway, you had the ticket last night – can't you remember what you did with it?'

'If I could we'd hardly be pulling the place apart looking for it.'

Gary muttered furiously as he emptied out drawers and rifled through their muddle. Marlene fumed as she inspected the contents of waste paper baskets and the rubbish bin. Galvanised into action by the possibility of an almost unimaginable prize, each continued to blame the other for the disappearance of the ticket and punctuated their search by shouting unreasonable and hateful accusations.

'My mother never wanted me to marry you – said you were a loser – and by God she was right!' Marlene teetered on a chair, peering into very unlikely cupboards and on top of grimy shelves.

Gary looked under some cushions for at least the fourth time. 'I couldn't give a monkey's what your mother thought – if she could think at all. Anyway, she produced a nice little slut in you.'

Marlene got down from her chair as swiftly as her very short tight skirt allowed. Her eyes blazed. 'I suppose that little tart called Daisy Latimer who you had an affair with had a house like Buckingham Palace?'

'Yeah, just the same.' There was a pause. 'I didn't know you knew about Daisy Latimer!'

'Course I bloody knew – you're not smart enough to cover up something like that from me. *And* I knew when she chucked you – couldn't blame her. Anyway, I was having it off with Kevin Marchant at the time.'

Gary's mouth dropped open. Marlene poked her face into his. 'You *are* a loser, Gary, like my Mum said. You're no good at keeping a job down, you're no good as a husband, you're no good in bed – and even if you think you've won the lottery you lose the damn ticket!'

Gary met his Waterloo. He was angry and frustrated about the elusive lottery ticket, and this triggered all the anger, frustration and even hatred which had been smouldering within him for years. It swelled and spurted out of him like lava from a volcano.

He grabbed Marlene's shoulders and shook her with all the force he could muster. She tried desperately and furiously to beat him with her fists and scratch him with her nails, but he was too strong for her. Then his big hands moved up to her throat. The more she struggled the tighter he squeezed. She made little choking sounds before she went limp and he let her fall to the floor.

He stared down at her – at first almost triumphant, then horrified and finally in terrified panic. His mouth desiccated and he began to tremble all over.

Murder in the course of robbery – that's what, he thought desperately. He'd been in the pub for a good time already tonight, as he usually was, and hopefully nobody would have noticed that he'd been missing for a while. He'd go back to the pub, then return to the flat, discover all this, be very distraught and send for the police. That's the plan – and no time to hang about.

He snatched his jacket from the floor and rushed out of the flat, shovelling his arms into sleeves as he skeltered down the stairs. In his ever-rising panic and haste he was uncoordinated. He lost his footing and flayed about in an attempt to regain his balance. But he failed. He somersaulted out of control and crashed headlong down the stone steps. There was a loud crack as his skull met the concrete beneath. His body lay spread-eagled and completely still. Slowly a pool of blood collected around it.

Back in the silent chaos which was the flat, the tabby cat yawned. She stood up, performed a back-arching stretch and jumped down from the chair.

In the still-warm place where her body had been curled was the lottery ticket.

The final number on it was 5.

12 ~ In Hiding

The dappled curve of the tiny fawn's body merged with fallen leaves and tall fading grasses. It was completely still. Some primeval instinct governed this stillness, its only defence against danger. The forest whispered around it, bathed in the burnt sienna of late afternoon sun. The fawn watched and waited for its mother's return.

The man was running fast through a path in the woods. He was wild-eyed and panting with effort. He repeatedly glanced behind him, terrified of any sight or sound of his pursuers. His fear governed his flight, and his adrenalin-fired body was pushing every muscle to its extreme limit and every sense into high alert. He knew if they caught him they would kill him. He must get to the border – then he would be safe.

The faun's acute hearing picked up an approaching sound. Its body sensed vibrations from the ground in increasing intensity. Still it remained immobile, only its large frightened eyes moving watchfully. The danger was coming nearer and nearer.

The fugitive thundered on. No sign of them yet – he might make it. He could just see the border in the distance now. This gave him hope and the hope spurred him on even more.

Then – disaster! His foot caught in a tree root and he was thrown to the ground with a heavy thud. There was a crack and an excruciating pain in his ankle. He groaned in pain and in despair – but he could not and would not lose his sense of extreme urgency and his instinct for self preservation. He rolled himself off the path and into the undergrowth which bordered it. He lay gasping for breath. How could he escape now? He couldn't run on an injured ankle. But all his effort must not end in futility.

The faun had heard danger coming nearer and louder and then a strange frightening creature had come into sight and crashed to the ground somewhere very close. The little animal was terrified – but still it instinctively knew not to run – to run would make it more vulnerable than ever. It lay there trembling, listening to the weird sounds that the creature was making.

The man rolled over. His ankle was hurting like hell. He looked around him. His vision was somewhat blurred, but lying there amongst the leaves he thought he could make out two brown eyes watching him through the grasses. He fleetingly wondered if in his desperate state he was hallucinating – but no – the eyes were in a head, and the head belonged to a miracle of camouflage. The frightened innocent eyes continued to stare at him and the small defenceless body was trembling in fear.

The man shuffled himself further away from the path, where the leaves were deeper – even in his extremis not wanting to disturb the little deer. He muttered half to himself and half to his fellow-in-hiding 'We seem to be in the same sort of boat – I reckon two can play at your game – and it's the only chance I've got.' He scooped out a dip as deep as he could in the accommodating leaves, rolled into it and then piled leaves on top of himself. It was reminiscent of burying himself in sand at the seaside. But all the time, with pounding heart, he listened for his pursuers. They were bound to come, although he was surprised that there had been quite as much distance between them.

The woods were quiet now and the fawn felt calmer and trembled less It could not see the strange creature any more, but its instinct told it that it was not very far away. It flattened its ears and tucked its head down to complete the circle of its body.

Then there was the danger noise again! This time it was louder and the vibrations greater.

Later than the fawn had heard the sounds, so did the man. They were very near now – men running hard and every now and then briefly shouting to each other in words that he could not understand. He thought that his thundering heart would burst within his chest. He willed the men to run past. He willed them not to notice the pile of leaves which was him. He also found himself willing them not to see the perfect little creature which was also in hiding. He prayed. Thoughts flashed through his head – of his childhood, of people important to him, past and present, of mowing grass, of Marmite on toast, of loving and of making love – and then of the terrible sequence of events that had led him to the here and now – in this foreign wood, hiding under a pile of leaves like a frightened animal.

The fawn felt the ground shaking as some more strange and noisy creatures approached. Wide-eyed it saw them tearing past. Scattered dust fell on its sensitive nose and into its eyes. But soon the disturbance was over.

They had gone past! Tension eased momentarily from the man's body, but still he lay motionless under his quilt of leaves. His pursuers had rushed off towards the border – but what then? They would not show themselves to the guard – would they assume that he was now out of their reach, or would they start searching for him in the woods? How could he know and what should he do next? His injured ankle was swelling inside his boot and was very painful, but he knew he must not take his boot off because he would never be able to get it on again and then he would be in a worse situation. His mouth was dust dry. He drained the last mouthfuls of water from his water bottle. He would wait and listen, wondering if the men would retrace their steps from the direction of the border.

The sun was setting now and shafts of light knifed through the trees and glowed on leaves and branches. Little seemed to move in the dappled forest although it was seething with secret life and providing a hiding place for the man and the tiny deer. Both bodies began to shiver as the sun lost its warmth.

Then there was noise and disturbance again. The men were indeed returning down the path! This time their pace was slower, but their voices still urgent and angry.

Once again they passed by. Once again the man was flooded with relief. He decided that he would wait for darkness and then make for the border as best he could – he had no other option. Then he heard a rustling from deeper in the forest. Fear struck again.

Had the men circled round and were looking for him from the other direction? But then he heard a soft animal sound. He peered through his leaf cover and saw, with strange delight that it was the hind – she had returned to her baby.

The little fawn heard its mother's call and with an answering sound was instantly on its feet. The man watched as mother and young nuzzled each other and the baby suckled gratefully before they disappeared into the forest.

As the sun slipped away it dragged with it the shafts of brightness between the trees. The glow on branches and foliage faded and the forest began to fill with the sounds of the night. The man rolled himself from his leafy couch and reached for a nearby stout stick, of which the forest floor offered a generous selection. Clinging to a tree trunk he managed to raise himself to standing, gathered another stick and with these makeshift crutches was able to propel himself along slowly. A pale crescent moon emerging fitfully from the clouds gave enough light to outline the trees and the path. Slowly and painfully and under cover of the blessed darkness the injured man struggled to the safety of the border.

Somewhere in the forest a little fawn was safe beside its mother.

And all was well.

13 ~ The Seven Deadly Sins

Envy, Pride, Sloth, Lust, Anger, Gluttony and Avarice. They lurk in dark places waiting to pounce out and try to possess us in moments of weakness. Sometimes we win and sometimes we lose – and then they go skulking off, to test us again – another time.

They are all here in this story, woven around an ordinary family.

Throw stones from your glass house if you dare!

* * * * *

'I'm moving in with Peter!' Kate informed her sister. They had met for a quick cup of coffee at the local Starbucks before Kate had to get back to the office and Amanda needed to return home to restore her house into some sort of order.

'That's great,' Amanda enthused, 'he's such a nice guy – you two should get on really well.'

'And his flat is nice too – I'm sure he won't mind me making a few changes – he's very easy-going. I'm moving in at the weekend!'

'Do Mum and Dad know?'

'No – I'll tell them tonight and we'll all see each other on Thursday, as we are coming to see your Harry in his school play.'

'Jake says he may not be able to make it,' Amanda said pensively, 'he seems very preoccupied work-wise at the moment.'

'Surely he'll come to see Harry?'

'Oh yes, I hope so – otherwise Harry will be so disappointed. I must rush off – heaps to do!' Amanda said, gulping the last mouthful of coffee and pushing her chair back.

'I'll pay for the coffee,' Kate said, 'see you on Thursday.'

'So pleased about Peter, Kate. Bye now.' And so the sisters parted, going their separate ways.

* * * * *

The following Saturday Kate arrived at Peter's flat. Her small car was crammed to capacity with her possessions – clothes still clinging to their hangers, plants with waving foliage and spilling earth, and boxes of half-used packets and jars of foodstuffs.

A couple of lamps balanced drunkenly on an assortment of books and magazines and a variety of bulging bags and baskets. Peter greeted Kate and her impedimenta with a cheerful and tolerant grin and proceeded to help her unload it all and pile it into the flat.

Stepping into the sitting room carrying a box of china and ornaments, Kate was struck by a golden tail-wagging, face-licking whirlwind. It was Bess, Peter's much –loved golden retriever. Kate managed to hang on to her box without too many of its contents spilling out before it reached the safety of the table. She had, of course, encountered Bess on many occasions, but this exuberant welcome made her realise with some force that she was not only moving in with Peter but also with Bess.

'She likes you,' laughed Peter, arriving behind a large plant in a pot the shape of a pig.

'Good,' said Kate, with as much enthusiasm as she could muster, looking ruefully at the paw marks on her pale blue tracksuit.

'Bess, on your bed!' commanded Peter. The dog reluctantly obeyed and watched as her master made two mugs of instant coffee and put them on the coffee table.

'Here's to us, then!' Peter raised his mug as if it were a glass of champagne and with his free hand pulled Kate's face towards him and kissed her. This was all too much for Bess, who had no wish at all to be confined to her bed and not be part of the proceedings. She wriggled up to Peter and Kate in great delight, wagging not only her tail but the whole of the rear part of her body. As she jumped up to share in the affectionate embrace, her swishing tail knocked Kate's coffee mug off the table, and the next quarter of an hour was spent trying to minimise damage to the carpet, the settee and Kate's beleaguered track suit.

Bess had not made a very good start to this ménage-a-tois. She clearly could not understand why and made such great play of being the injured party that Peter took her for a good long walk, leaving Kate to settle in the flat.

So that was how things began, and even then Kate felt a small twinge of resentment, which she brushed hastily aside. It was going to be lovely living with Peter – they would get on really well.

And so it was and so they did. But there was Bess. Whenever they went out in the car Bess lolled about in the back. She liked, if she got the chance, to sleep on the bed. She took up most of the room on the settee. She had to have her walks, come rain or shine. She often had special meals cooked for her in case tinned dog food lacked variety or proper nourishment. She chewed at Kate's plants and salivated on her slippers and the vacuum cleaner was put into overdrive sucking up her golden hairs which seemed to moult from her constantly. Her devotion to Peter was absolute She gazed at him with adoring brown eyes and drooling fixation. All right, dogs were like that, but what Kate found harder to come to terms with was that Peter's devotion to Bess seemed equally unquestioning and complete. Surely she couldn't be envious? Not of a dog – that would be ridiculous!

A few weeks later some friends of Kate's invited her and Peter to visit them. 'Liz and Jeff would like us to spend a weekend with them.' Kate told Peter.

'That's nice of them – where do they live?'

'In the New Forest – quite a small village.'

'Great! Good dog walking country!'

'We couldn't take Bess because one of their children gets asthma if a dog is in the house.'

'That's a shame – can't go then.'

'What do you mean we can't go – surely Bess can go to the kennels or to your parents or something for a weekend?'

'The parents are going away for a month shortly – and I can't put Bess in kennels – she'd hate it – you know she would.'

'So you won't go, just because of the dog?'

'No. I can't.'

'I'll go on my own then. You put that dog before anything else – certainly before me.'

There, she had said it. She couldn't help it – it just came out. Before Peter could answer she rushed out of the room to phone Liz and tell her that she would be coming for the weekend by herself.

Later in bed, Peter asked, 'When are you going to stay with Liz and Jeff?'

'The weekend after next.'

'Oh, right.'

'Peter, I'm sorry about what I said, I didn't really mean it.' – although in her heart she really felt that she had meant it. 'I don't want anything to come between us.' That, she knew, was true.

'Nor do I,' Peter said, reaching out for her, 'but I don't think that what I feel for Bess is out of proportion – I've had her for five years now and of course I am very fond of her and you can't expect me to change that – but she is a dog and you – are – well you – and I love you.'

'And Bess is part of the package?

'Something like that.' he said softly, pulling her towards him. 'She has completely accepted you here and anyone who is OK. for me, is OK. for her. Can't we just share her?'

'Of course,' she whispered putting the dog out of her mind.

But not for long, as very soon there was a great thump on the bed and a cold wet nose on their faces. Bess, finding the bedroom door not completely closed, was delighted to wriggle through it and claim her favourite sleeping place.

* * * * *

A few days later Kate was on the phone to Amanda.

'How are you Kate – and how's your lovely man?' asked Amanda.

'I'm OK. and the lovely man is OK. – but I have a rival and that's not really OK. I'm seriously wondering if this relationship will work – it is, to quote Princess Di, – a bit crowded.'

'What! Do you mean he has another girl?'

No – I think it would be almost more straightforward if he had. It's a dog.'

'A *dog*?'

'Yes – a large, over affectionate, all-invading golden retriever. She hasn't an ounce of malice in her and Peter absolutely adores her – but she somehow gets between us (sometimes quite literally) and, after all, she was here first.'

'Kate, you're being really stupid,' Amanda said in her elder sister voice, 'do you mean to say that you are jealous – of a *dog*? She sounds lovely. For goodness sake, get things in proportion.'

'I know it sounds silly and I do love Peter – he is kind and loving and tolerant and all the right things – but I just find it difficult sharing him with his dog. She's not *our* dog – she's *his* dog. If she was another woman I could at least have a confrontation – but you can't have a confrontation with a soft-as-butter dog who just puts a paw up and gazes at you with reproachful brown eyes. She is as tolerant as her master.'

'It all sounds a bit ridiculous to me', came the elder sister voice again,' I think that you are behaving rather like a spoilt child. Don't do anything you might regret.'

The phone clicked. Bess stood up in her bed, shook the usual ration of hairs out of her coat and flopped down again. Kate knew that she was getting restless as it was past the time that Peter usually arrived home and took her out for a run in the park. Often, work permitting, he was able to take Bess with him to work but today was not one of those days. Then the phone rang again. This time the dog sensed that it was her master's voice at the other end. Her ears cocked up and her tail thumped rhythmically on the floor.

I've got a bit held up here,' Peter was saying, 'be a darling and take Bess out for her run would you? I should be home within the hour. Love you! Bye now.'

Dusk was approaching and a light rain was beginning to fall. A walk in the park was at the bottom of Kate's priority list. She had not finished unpacking the shopping she had hastily gathered on her way home, let alone stared to prepare any supper. She hadn't even had a cup of tea. Whilst Bess whimpered in anticipation she shrugged herself into Peter's all-enveloping anorak.

'Come then, Bess!' she said unnecessarily, as Bess was already making a dive for the front door. 'Just a very quick walkies – and I'm not sure as if we shall be doing this for very much longer.'

* * * * *

Amanda had put the phone down rather crossly. How could her sister be so small-minded as to envy a dog and let it spoil a relationship with such a nice man? She shrugged her shoulders and returned to the chaos in the kitchen where the children and two of their friends were having tea.

Later, when the children were bathed, bedded and read to and some supper for herself and Jake was in the oven, she flopped in an armchair and flicked on the television. She watched the moving images on the screen without really seeing them. Jake was late. He was so often late these days and came home tired and grumpy.

Since he had left his previous firm and started up a business on his own with his colleague Mike, he had worked very long hours. The business seemed to be going quite well now, but it was at a price – it consumed all Jake's time and energy and he had less time for her and the children. She had been very upset that he had not managed to come to see Harry in his school play the other week because he had to go to Leicester and was not back in time. Why could he not have gone to Leicester another day and avoided disappointing Harry? The togetherness which she and Jake had enjoyed was diminishing, and she had to admit to feelings of resentment. This was unreasonable, she told herself – Jake was working hard for the benefit of the family.

It's a bit like Jane and Peter and the dog, she thought, engendering a degree of empathy after all, for her sister.

The front door slammed, heralding Jake's arrival home.

'You're late!' Amanda greeted him accusingly.

'I know I'm late – it's not necessary for you to point it out,' Jake retorted, pouring himself a drink. 'Want one?'

'No, I've had a couple while I've been waiting for you. I expect the supper is rather dried up'.

'Never mind – I'm not hungry – I got a take-away sent in and had it in the office.'

'You might have let me know.'

'Sorry, didn't think, I was too busy trying to clinch a deal with this chap in Japan. I'm turning in shortly, I've got an early start tomorrow.'

Later they lay in bed, not touching one another.

'Jake, you can't go on working all the hours God gives. I feel that our family life is suffering.'

'What d'you mean?' Jake grunted sleepily. He felt tired and irritated and had no wish to enter into any sort of discussion or argument.

'Well,' continued Amanda, 'you know how disappointed Harry was that you didn't get that concert he was in. That sort of thing. You haven't enough time for us.'

'I'm working my socks off at the business. Can't perform miracles. You and the kids seem OK. What more d'you expect?'

'A better family life – that's what! Now that the business has got off the ground can't you afford some secretarial help or something?

'Mm – might be a good idea.'

'Why don't you put an advertisement in the local paper?

'I'll talk to Mike in the morning,' Jake muttered in an 'end of conversation' tone, humped himself further down into the duvet and was instantly asleep.

However, the following week an advertisement did indeed appear in the local paper.

Small busy local firm requires secretarial help.
Computer skills an advantage.
Hours and salary by arrangement.
Please contact Jake Somerton or Michael May.

Tel:- 01679 557682.

* * * * *

Madeline, sitting on her white settee in her immaculate sitting room, saw the advertisement and carefully made a note of the telephone number. She thought that getting a job of this sort may help her to cope with the mess her life had got itself into.

The last months for her had been a nightmare. It had begun when she returned from the hairdressers one afternoon all primped and manicured, to find her husband Gary surprisingly at home. His large frame was slumped in an armchair and in his hand was a half-full glass of whisky which was in imminent danger of being spilt on the floor.

'Gary!' Madeline exclaimed, 'What are you doing here at this time of day? And look out – you're about to spill that drink on the carpet – and you know that I like you to take your shoes off before you come into the sitting room!'

'Anything else?' slurred Gary.

'Yes – you've been drinking – and what *are* you doing home at this time in the afternoon?'

'I am home, my loving wife, because I have no need to be anywhere else. It was tactfully explained to me today that Rodborough Atkinson and Longshanks Patent Company no longer require my services.'

'What! Do you mean that you've got the sack?'

'To put it in more vulgar terms – yes.'

'But they can't do that – you must sue for unfair dismissal!'

'I could, but I don't think it would get me very far – only on the wrong side of a pile of legal fees. I bungled several applications over the last year with rather disastrous consequences. Old Rodborough was very pissed off about it – and his particularly pious and irritating son charmingly told me that I was a lazy bastard. Lazy I may be but bastard I am not and I have my birth certificate to prove it.'

'Gary, don't try and be funny. This is quite dreadful. What are you going to do – and what are our friends going to think?'

'Can't say I know the answer to either of those questions. I suppose I'll think of something – and our friends can think what they damn well like.'

'We mustn't let the neighbours know that you've lost your job,' prattled Madeline urgently, '– we shall say that you are now working from home – lots of people do that now.'

'Oh, – that'll be cosy.' Gary smirked at her.

'And what, pray, do you think we're going to do for money?'

'Well, you have your money and I shall get three months salary – so we'll be OK. for a while.'

'And then what? We can't keep up our lifestyle and live in this house if you don't have a job.'

'I expect something will crop up.'

'That's you all over – just wait for 'something to crop up' – as long as you don't have to make any effort about it yourself. Well, something may just not crop up and then where shall we be?'

'Oh – don't take on so woman. Anyway, for the time being I shall enjoy not going off every morning to that bloody office.'

'You'll have to 'sign on' – or whatever they call it now at the Job Centre. I hope nobody we know sees you there!'

'I can rely on you to worry more about what the neighbours think than about me losing my job. If I go to the Job Centre I'll go in disguise.'

Madeline took the glass out of her slouching husband's hand and placed it on a coaster on the highly polished table. 'Very funny,' she almost sneered, 'I'll look out for a false beard at the joke shop.' And with that she stormed out of the room.

Gary stirred himself sometime later and ambled off to the pub. He returned when the pub closed even more the worse for wear. He crashed out asleep on the settee fully clothed, except that this time he had taken his shoes off.

The weeks that followed were very difficult. Madeline was not enjoying having Gary at home all the time. He got up late, idled about in his dressing gown for the rest of the morning and just about managed to get dressed by lunchtime. Lunchtime! That was a bone of contention. Madeline didn't 'do' lunchtime – except, that was, when she gave one of her nice little lunch parties – which she couldn't do now, with Gary lurking about.

She was often invited out to lunch herself or enjoyed a meal with a friend in town and perhaps had a shopping spree or went to a matinee. Providing lunch for a hungry husband every day was certainly not on the curriculum which she was used to and went very much against the grain. She was far too proud to tell the neighbours that she had an out-of-work husband, or convey the fact to her friends, so there was the constant pretence to be kept up that Gary was 'working from home.' One of her neighbours encountered him in his dressing gown late one morning and she had to explain that he had had a bad bout of 'flu and that it would be inadvisable for anyone to venture into the house. She also had to keep making up reasons to decline invitations and not to offer hospitality. Worrying about money, what everyone would think and the reduction in their lifestyle was making her feel quite ill – not to mention her exasperation with Gary, ho seemed to be making very little effort to find another job. Madeline plied him with newspapers and printed out job opportunities from the internet to no avail. Finally she had to admit to herself that he was completely and utterly idle, and what love she had had for him was rapidly evaporating. When she had first met him she thought him attractive, amusing, fun to be with and easy-going. When he asked her if she would marry him she really thought that they could be happy together. For his part he found her pretty, sexy and very feminine and the fact that he knew that a great aunt had left her, her only niece, a very nice house and a small legacy was an added attraction.

Eventually Miranda insisted that Gary applied for Unemployment Benefit and he had to frequent the Job Centre.

'We can't manage just on my investment income now your money from the company has stopped,' she said to him one morning, looking at him disapprovingly as he was stretched out on the settee reading James Bond, 'you'll have to get some sort of job. It is bound not to be as well paid as your last one, so I think I shall have to see if I can find one as well even if it is only part-time.

'I don't suppose you'll like that much,' responded Gary, not raising his eyes from his book, ' that would get in the way of your social round. I wish you didn't think it is so important to keep up with the Jones's and want money to spend on the house and yourself all the time, and be able to outdo your neighbours and friends as far as holidays are concerned. And there's all this silly nonsense about pretending I'm working from home. You're just too *proud* Madeline, *and* you're a snob. Why can't we just scale down our spending a bit?'

Madeline was incensed. 'Because I don't want to, that's why,' she screeched, heedless for once, as to whether the neighbours heard or not, 'I am entitled to my life-style and I don't want to change it – and I don't want to look a fool in front of everyone and for them to know that I am married to an idle lay-about. I don't want to be *pitied*!'

Guy walked out of the room before he hit Madeline He went upstairs, shovelled himself into some old clothes and set off for the Job Centre, slamming the door very loudly behind him, not caring who heard or who saw him.

He was sitting waiting in the Job Centre when a cheerful-looking youth strode in. He was the elder son of the family next door. He greeted Gary with ill-disguised but friendly surprise. He had just come down from university and was wanting a fill-in job to earn some money before he went away for a year. As they sat and chatted Gary realized that this encounter would put the cat amongst the pigeons.

And it did. It was not long before the boy's mother, bumping into Madeline in the butchers shop had to learn that the 'working from home' arrangement had not been as satisfactory as had been hoped. Madeline was mortified. Now, of course, everyone would know. She wished that she had not lied about it all in the first place.

The relationship between Madeline and Gary deteriorated daily until it was impossible for them to be civil to each other.

'You have turned into a nagging, house-proud fishwife,' Gary shouted at her one morning. 'I'm fed up with you worrying about what people are thinking about you all the time – it's a pathetic way of going on.'

'Its you who's the pathetic one,' Madeline retorted, 'you don't care about me, you don't care about not having a job – you are bone idle. Did you know that a sloth moves so slowly that lichens and moss have time to grow on its fur – well, if you look in the mirror one day and you look a bit green you will know why.'

'We can't go on like this,' said Gary, 'I'll ring my sister and see if I can go and stay with them until I sort something out – that'd be better that staying here. You can stuff your house and your high and mighty ideas and I'll be happy to get out of your hair.'

Madeline sighed as she thought back on those unhappy months. But now she must look forward – and she carefully dialled the telephone number to enquire about the job advertised in the local paper

Jake and his business partner Mike received three responses to their newspaper advertisement and they interviewed each applicant. Sadie was officious and somewhat intimidating,

Gloria cheerful but completely inexperienced and very sloppy-looking with hair like a bottle brush and chipped purple varnish on her nails. Madeline was smart, attractive, sensible and friendly and seemed the obvious choice. She was pleased to accept the job and was available to commence work straight away.

By the end of a fortnight Jake and Mike wondered however they had managed without Madeline. Orders were pouring in and the business was running like clockwork.

* * * * *

'You're late again,' Amanda complained one evening when Jake arrived home to a microwaved supper, 'I thought that now you had some help in the office you would be home earlier.'

'On the whole I have been,' said Jake, kicking his shoes off, 'but tonight we wanted to get some paperwork finished and Madeline stayed on to do it – she is very obliging.'

'Well,' Amanda continued in her complaining voice, 'I really needed you this evening. Something has gone wrong with my car again and its refusing to start. As you weren't here I had to get taxi to collect Alice from dancing. It was ages coming so by the time I arrived she was in tears.'

'Sorry darling, you should have phoned me.'

'I did, but I suppose that the obliging Madeline didn't pass on the message.'

Jake grunted and began to consume his not especially appetising supper. He looked at Amanda who, in her dressing gown and slippers, was disconsolately doing some ironing in front of the television. She could do with a new car, he thought. The business is doing fairly well now and he should be able to afford it. Perhaps he could get one and give it to her as a surprise – might cheer her up, she seems a bit down and difficult to approach lately.

On his way to the office the following morning Jake went into the local car salesroom, where new and nearly new cars stood in gleaming expectant rows. An eager salesman jumped out at him like a spider coming out of its web.

'Can I help you, Sir?'

'Well, I am on the lookout for a car for my wife – suitable for general family use. Hatchback probably – not a great lumbering 4x4, she won't be crashing through Africa.'

The salesman delighted in embarking on discourses about various models of vehicles until Jake felt it was a mistake to get involved in the proceedings any further before getting to the office. He said he would come back at a more appropriate time and returned to his car clutching a number of glossy brochures.

In his office Madeline was busy on the computer.

'Sorry I'm a bit late,' Jake said somewhat unnecessarily. 'I popped into Charlston Motors on the way in. My wife needs a new car.'

'Lucky her!' said Madeline, involuntarily wishing that she had a husband intent on buying her a new car

'I thought that I might give it to her as a surprise.'

'Even luckier her!' said Madeline, clambering up on a chair in order to look for something in a high cupboard.

'I'll get up there for you,' said Jake hurriedly, 'what is it you want?'

'It's OK. – I can reach it – a new packet of computer paper.' Jake found that he didn't mind Madeline not getting down from her perch on the chair.

He looked at her neat bottom and her shapely legs and her very feminine and ridiculously impractical shoes. And he liked what he saw.

* * * * *

The next time Amanda and Kate met each other for lunch the conversation very quickly centred around the situation between Kate and Peter.

'Well,' Amanda said in a demanding tone, 'have you sorted things out in your head about Peter and the hound?'

'Yes, I have,' Kate said, with a sad and somewhat guilty look at her sister.

Amanda leant forward and stared at Kate. 'Tell me all,' she said, cupping her face in her hands.

Kate screwed her nose up miserably. 'I felt worse about it after the weekend when Peter didn't come with me to stay with my friends Liz and Jeff who live in the New Forest. One of their children has asthma and they cannot have dogs around the place and Peter wouldn't go without Bess. He wouldn't put her in kennels because he says she would hate it and his parents couldn't have her because they were going away. So I went on my own. I would so have liked Liz and Jeff to have met Peter – but they didn't – all because of the dog. I told Peter that he puts the dog before anything else – certainly before me And he didn't like that and I got all upset and cried and said that we had better not go on living together. Its all very miserable.' Tears sprang into Kate's eyes and began to trickle down her face.

'I still think that you have got it out of proportion, said Amanda, providing her sister with a paper handkerchief, 'and what would you do if you moved out of Peter's flat – you've lost your other flat now.'

'I could probably share my friend Jill's flat until I sort myself out as her flat mate has gone to the States for a year and she would probably be glad of the rent.'

'And what about all your stuff? Our garage is full to bursting – so don't bank on us for storage. Anyway – that's all by the way compared with the feelings that you and Peter have for each other. I think that you are being obsessional and silly. To be jealous of a dog is ridiculous. I said it before and I say it again. Peter is such a nice man – and any relationship must have its give and take.'

Kate looked gloomily out of the window, watching people hurrying by – people with no problems – with houses to live in, with happy relationships and with no dogs to take their places in other's hearts. 'That's enough about me,' she said, 'how are things with you? Is Jake still working all hours?'

'Well, They have got a girl helping in the office now Jake says that she is very obliging - whatever that may mean!

Anyway, we don't seem to have much time to talk like we used to – he is wrapped up in the business and I am so busy with the children and their schools and the Parent/Teachers things and the house and the garden and the couple of committees I'm on, as well as keeping an eye on my two elderly neighbours. I don't seem to have time to do anything for *me* – things I would really *like* to do. And my car keeps letting me down. Sometimes I feel so *tired,* Kate. I caught sight of myself in a shop window coming along today – and I looked really old and frumpy!'

'Oh dear!' exclaimed Kate, 'you and Jake have always seemed fine for each other. Can I come over and stay with the children so that you can have an evening out more often?'

'An evening out?' You must be joking! Jake comes home too late and too tired and the last thing on the agenda would be an evening out. As you know, he didn't even get to that play which Harry was in – who was, of course, very upset and disappointed.'

'I expect that exercised the give and take thing,' said Kate.

Amanda smiled ruefully as they both left the café, each weighted down with their own problems.

* * * * *

Jake and Mike were discussing a business concern in Manchester. 'I think that it would be a good idea if you accepted the invitation to attend that meeting next week, Jake,' said Mike, 'there's nothing quite like talking to people face to face.'

'I suppose you're right,' answered Jake, 'd'you think it would be OK. to be away from the office for a couple of days at the moment?'

'Oh yes – I have got that chap coming to talk about the Rendells order and then amongst other things I have to visit Palmers and see what is going on there – that doesn't need two of us. What about asking Madeline if she would go with you? She's very good at taking notes etc. and she always seems to be able to put her hands on the right bits of paperwork. She'd be quite an asset. We can just rely on the answer phone and e-mail here if nobody is in the office – we always used to!'

It struck Jake as a very good idea to ask Madeline if she could go to Manchester with him. Subsequently, it struck Madeline as a very good idea also.

Jake arranged to meet Madeline at the City Airport. He had not been waiting long when he saw her coming through the entrance doors. She was looking incredibly attractive in a black silky trouser-suit with a white revered blouse, which gave a tantalising hint of her cleavage. Once settled on the plane they chatted about the forthcoming meetings.

However much Jake was anxious to further his business interests he found it surprisingly difficult to concentrate on them completely. He was so acutely conscious of the physical presence of Madeline beside him, leaning, just slightly towards him – of her perfume, of the touch of her arm against his, of the softness of her pretty face and of her utter femininity. 'God help me, he thought, I want to go to bed with her!'

Madeline, for her part, was, of course, perfectly aware of this fact and by behaving as if she was not, was increasing her desirability.

The meeting that day went fairly well and they were discussing it over a very enjoyable dinner at the hotel.

'Thanks for being willing to come with me Madeline,' Jake said, refilling her wine glass, 'you're a great help.'

'Pleasure!' Madeline said, smiling at him over her glass. 'It's a nice change to come away somewhere – and I've never been to Manchester before.'

'Like to sample some Manchester nightlife?'

'Love to!'

Jake had not been to a Night Club for years. He felt excited and rather like a naughty boy. He thought guiltily of Amanda and rang her on his mobile. She was cross that he had not rung earlier and why was his mobile turned off when she had tried to ring him? – and anyway she was almost asleep because she had had a very busy day. He said that he hoped she would sleep well, that the meeting went OK. and that he would be home tomorrow evening. He then met Madeline in the hotel foyer, put a protective arm around her and hailed a taxi.

Jake did not particularly enjoy the Night Club – he found it claustrophobic and noisy and he reluctantly accepted this attitude as a sign of middle age. What he did enjoy was smooching around in a corner of the small dance floor holding Madeline very close indeed, regardless of the fact that most other revellers seemed intent on performing some crazy sort of corroboree. To Jake, Madeline felt delicious and his whole body ached with desire for her. He liked her very much, but was not in love with her – he recognised that his desire was fuelled by an urgent and desperate lust and he felt both guilty and exhilarated.

They arrived back at the hotel relaxed and laughing. Madeline was dangling her shoes from one hand and some of her fair hair had escaped from its retaining clasp. She looked deliciously childlike and slightly dishevelled.

'Thank you – boss!' She giggled as Jake opened the door of her room for her.

'There's just one more request the boss would like to make of the secretary tonight,' he said, '– invite me in for a nightcap?'

'Willingly,' whispered his accomplice.

* * * * *

On a Friday some weeks later Kate, who had an extra day off, was having coffee in Amanda's kitchen. After a somewhat disorganised breakfast the rest of the family had all bundled off – Jake to his office and the children to school and the sisters were sitting amidst a familiar trail of debris which had been left in their wake.

'My week's been pretty awful', volunteered Amanda, 'how about yours?'

'Horrid,' replied Kate, who was ready to burst into tears, 'I miss Peter terribly, and he hasn't phoned all week. I shouldn't have moved out should I?'

'No,' her sister replied uncompromisingly, 'although I began to understand a little bit how you felt.'

'Really? I'm glad about that – but it doesn't make any difference to the here and now! How are you and Jake and the children?'

'Much the same. Of course I am pleased that the business is doing well now and it is silly of me to feel resentful that it takes up all his time and energy and I feel sort of left out – a bit like you and Peter and Bess – only we're all people – and Bess is only a dog! Jake seems more detached than grumpy these days, but he is still working very long hours. I thought it might have got better now they have this part-time secretary – but sometimes he gets home even later than ever. He was away in Manchester two days the other week. I think that all went OK. because he seemed to come back on a bit of a high – but we haven't had much time to talk about it, in fact we don't seem to communicate like we used to – I suppose its just family life – which kind of takes you over. We used to talk a lot in bed – but now we just crash out to sleep. No talk, no sex, just sleep. Anyway, at least this morning Jake has taken the children off to school as my car is playing up again. Jake says I really need a new one – but he hasn't had time to do anything about it. I will have to borrow his tomorrow to get the children to the various things they get up to on Saturdays – there's karate for Harry, swimming for Charlie and riding for Alice.'

'We didn't do all these out of school things did we?' said Kate, helping herself to another cup of coffee.

'No, – p'raps Dad didn't want to pay for them – he always has been – I won't say actually *mean* – but not exactly one to throw his money about. But then again, there wasn't this plethora of activities going on for kids – their friends do this that and the other, so they want to as well, and you don't want them to feel left out – so life ends up more of a scramble than ever, with everyone exhausted – especially me!'

'Oh dear,' sighed Kate.

Returning to Peter, – don't you think you will get back with him?' asked Amanda, fingering a sticky marmalade jar.

'I've probably messed it all up for good now,' Kate said, rubbing her tears away and smearing eye make-up all over her face. 'I don't want to talk about it any more. What a nuisance about your car. Cars are such a boon when they go and such a bore when they don't' she said with a sympathetic smile. 'Anyway, I must go and do a bit of shopping. Hope your weekend is OK. I was going to see Mum and Dad and Marcus but they had something on, so I'm going next weekend instead.'

Marcus had made a surprising arrival in the family many years after his sisters and had always been indulged by all.

Kate kissed her sister and let herself out of the house and Amanda resignedly turned her attention to the kitchen.

* * * * *

After the trip to Manchester Jake and Madeline had arranged clandestine meetings, mostly at Madeline's house. She had been separated from Gary for some time now and Amanda's enthusiasm for lovemaking had clearly waned, so Jake and Madeline gloriously met each other's sex-starved needs. Jake tried to make excuses for himself but had a constant deep nagging guilt. He knew that he ought to stop having sex with Madeline and probably persuade her to find another job, but she was so soft and willing and desirable. When she was in the office he would fantasize about being in bed with her. When he was lying next to the unresponsive sleeping Amanda he couldn't help wishing that he was beside Madeline whom he could pull towards him and make love to. He was a bit like a child having access to some forbidden chocolate biscuits and was compelled to put its hand in the cookie jar 'just one more time.' Then he wondered how he could be so unfaithful and devious and so completely lacking in any self control. But he seemed incapable of stopping himself.

Perhaps it was partly to assuage his guilt that he carefully chose a very nice brand new car for Amanda. He had arranged for it to be delivered to the office car park and then to drive it home as a surprise for her.

Jake was unaware of the fact that his partner Mike's mother-in–law lived in the same area as Madeline and was often visited by her daughter Janet.

'Mike,' said Janet over supper to her husband one evening, 'does Jake still have his blue BMW?'

'Yes, why?'

'Because I see it from time to time in the drive of a house in Tudor Avenue which I pass on the way to Mum's.'

'That's Madeline Pritchard's house – my mate Amy lives over the road from her,' piped up their sharp-eared twelve year-old daughter Sophie.

Mike instantly changed the subject by piling some more vegetables onto Sophie's plate and telling her to eat them because they were good for her, to which she protested loudly.

But the damage was done. Gossip travels like a spark along an explosives wire. Then there is the explosion. Sophie told Amy, Amy told her mother – who just happened to 'mention it' to a friend – who knew someone who went to an evening class with a person who worked with an acquaintance of Amanda's. This person, in the guise of a 'well wishing friend', with an expression of studied anguish on her face had told all the gossip which she had heard to Amanda herself. They had met at the pedestrian crossing in the High Street. Amanda was not going to give the bringer of these tidings the satisfaction of witnessing any of the emotion she felt. She gave rather a grim smile as if husbands' adultery was not much more than one could expect and hurried off in the opposite direction. She drove home in a daze and slumped down in an armchair with a stiff drink.

Could it be true? Perhaps it was just malicious gossip? But then her racing thoughts told her that it could just be true – things had not been good between her and Jake for some time and although she tried to stop them, all sorts of thoughts slithered and scrambled about in her head.

The seed had been sown. For a while she put herself in a state of denial. Jake couldn't possibly be having an affair with the 'obliging' Madeline– but then could he be?

Serious doubts began to drip feed into her head. Had she heard the classic 'I'll be working late tonight' statement rather too often? Were the now regular Friday night flowers produced for the wrong reason? Why did he opt out of spending a weekend with her family recently? Did he really have a 'lad's night' at a pub some ten miles away last Tuesday?

Perhaps she was just being unreasonably suspicious? She shouldn't have taken notice of gossip.

But then the next day she found them – in the pocket of his business suit – two theatre ticket stubs for one of the nights when he was supposed to be at an evening conference in London.

No wonder his answer phone was turned off!

Instinctively now, she realised the truth. Jake and that tart of a secretary! She then let her emotions take full reign – shock, resentment, guilt, betrayal, but most of all anger. She felt enveloped in a suffocating red blanket of anger. She had a compulsion to confront Jake immediately. She couldn't wait until she heard his key in the lock – and anyway by then the children would be around. How could he do this to the children? How dare he do this to her and the children!

She rushed out of the house and flung herself into her old car. It spluttered protestingly into life and she drove to Jake's office.

There, in the small car park stood two cars. Mike's old family Volvo wasn't there and sitting next to Jake's BMW was a smart new Peugeot.

'*Her's* she hissed to herself, 'well she's not going to like this very much!'

She opened the boot of Jake's car and took out the large spanner which he kept there in case he had to change a wheel. In a blaze of uncontrollable anger which seared into her head and her heart, she furiously scraped the heavy spanner all round the pristine paintwork of the Peugeot. She then whammed the spanner onto one of the windows, which made a satisfying crash as it crumbled into small pieces which scattered and clattered to the ground. She was just about to repeat the process on another window, when Jake, having heard the noise, came rushing out.

'Amanda!' he shrieked, 'What the hell are you doing? I've just bought you that bloody car!'

Amanda, the outraged wife, spanner in hand, stared at her outraged husband. And then she opened her mouth and screamed and screamed as she had never screamed before.

* * * * *

That Saturday Kate went to see her parents. She found them in a state of considerable agitation.

'Whatever's the matter, Mum?' asked Kate, as her mother's worried face greeted her at the door.

'It's Marcus.' her mother replied, kissing her absently and wiping her eyes.

'Yes, you told me that he had been sent home from school because he had been sick.'

But he's been so *ill* Kate.'

'What sort of ill?' Kate wanted to know.

'The school asked us to bring him home as he had been very sick and faint. Oh Kate, he looked absolutely dreadful – I thought he was going to die. He went on being sick and so we sent for the doctor of course, but he couldn't come so we had to take him to the hospital – to Casualty.'

'And what did they say?'

'They said that it was probably a very bad tummy upset. They said that he didn't have appendicitis. They took some samples and are going to let us know about the results of those in a few days. Then they said we could take him home and keep him quiet. The poor darling could hardly walk, so we put him in a wheelchair to take him back to the car.'

'Poor old chap,' said Kate feelingly, 'and how is he now?'

'Not at all himself – I really feel that the doctor should come and see him – but they aren't keen to do home visits these days. I think it's awful. He looks so pale and doesn't want to get out of bed. We are still very worried about him and think that something in the school dinner has given him food poisoning. That can be very serious, you know. Your father has been to see the headmaster to complain and is threatening to sue. I am sterilising everything that goes in and out of his room.'

'Oh Mum, don't let Dad get involved with suing – it may well be more trouble than it's worth – as long as Marcus will be OK. – that's all that matters.'

'Well, you know what Dad's like when he gets his teeth into something. Especially if there is money involved.'

'Yes, I do – and *especially* if there's money involved. I'm going up to see Marcus.'

Marcus was lying listlessly in bed. He was surrounded by unread books and ignored model-making activities. A series of muffled discordant squeaks came from the earphones which he had clamped to his ears. Kate walked softly into the room.

'Hello, Marky, how are you feeling?' she asked.

Marcus turned his pale plump face towards her and dislodged his earphones.

'Awful,' he answered, 'I think I've got food poisoning, and don't suppose I'll live.'

'Don't be so silly,' rejoined his sister, 'you'll probably be as right as ninepence tomorrow.'

'How can you know? Mum and Dad are very worried about me.'

'Mum will worry about you at the drop of a hat, and Dad is always game for a bit of confrontation and demanding his rights. He has already gone to the school and threatened that he will sue the Education Authority for poisoning the school dinners.'

On hearing this remark Kate noticed a look of alarm spread over Marcus's face.

'He can't do that!'

'Oh, why not? You know what Dad's like – and think what you could do if he wins some compensation money- that is, of course, if you live to receive it.'

'B-b-but,' stammered the bulk in the bed, disappearing under its duvet.

'I'll go now, I expect you need lots of rest,' Kate said, as she left the room.

Her parents were both in the kitchen and the atmosphere was anything but joyful. Her mother was crying and her father looked angry. As Kate was putting her arm around her mother to comfort her, the door bell rang and she hurried to open it.

There stood a red-eyed distraught Amanda.

'My God, Amanda – whatever's happened?' Kate bustled her sister into the kitchen where she promptly slumped into a chair, burst into yet more tears and in between her sobs gave a rather disjointed account about Jake's affair and the disaster concerning the car.

They all stared at Amanda in horror and then her mother let out a wail. 'Everything's going wrong with our family- its all horrible – Kate and Peter, now Amanda's marriage, dear Marcus is upstairs so ill and Dad's all set to get involved with the law. Nothing is going right – whatever shall we do?'

'Somehow we shall sort it out,' said her husband grimly.

Later that day, Kate had left to go to the theatre with a girl-friend, Amanda had gone to collect her children from various activity venues and Marcus, surrounded by cushions and comforts was ensconced on the settee with his Game Boy, mesmerized by the crazed moving images on the television screen.

The parents were finishing their supper in the kitchen in a somewhat distracted fashion, as their minds were dwelling on their children's problems.

'Oh Geoffrey,' said Linda miserably, 'Whatever is happening to our family? However could Amanda and Jake's marriage have got into such a mess? I thought everything was going all right for them. What effect is all this going to have on the children? Oh dear! Oh *dear!* And we can't do much to help, with poor Marcus so ill.'

Geoffrey stroked his balding head 'We shall just have to hope that they will be able to sort things out between them – they both seem to have been under pressure lately.'

'They probably could do with some time on their own and a chance to talk. Perhaps later on we could offer to look after the children? But Jake is so wrapped up in his business that he mightn't be able to get away.'

'That's probably part of the trouble,' said Geoffrey, helping himself to some more cheese and biscuits, 'they seem to be OK financially – and that's always important.'

'I often don't think it has the amount of importance than you think it has.'

'Of course it has!'

'And then there's Kate,' continued Linda, 'she hasn't looked happy ever since she and that nice Peter parted company. I never quite understood what happened there.'

'No, and I don't suppose we need to. There's nothing we can do about that – but there is something we can do about Marcus – I'm out for compensation over this food poisoning business. People get compensation for all sorts of things these days – and often amazing amounts of money. I've already spoken to the headmaster at the school – he knows I'm on the warpath. I'll make an appointment to see the solicitor tomorrow. One of my mate's has told me about one who is hot stuff on compensation cases – pricey, but effective. We may be in line for a nice little windfall.'

'Oh Geoffrey, must you go on with that? I don't think that it would be very good for Marcus – and what happens if the case falls through?'

'We don't get any money – but it's worth a good try.'

'Well I don't think it is,' Linda sighed as she went into the sitting room to make sure that pressing his Game Boy buttons was not being too much of a strain for Marcus.

* * * * *

A few days later Geoffrey was sitting at a desk in an expensive-looking office opposite a suave and self-confident youngish solicitor, Mr Ponsonby of Stemson, Muncaster & Ponsonby.

'Well, Mr Broadbent, I have studied the information I have concerning your complaint against the school and your son's sickness.'

'You mean his food poisoning,' interjected Geoffrey quickly.

'We cannot call it food poisoning until we are sure of the facts.'

'Of course we have the facts – Marcus had his usual breakfast with us – and there was nothing the matter with that – and then in the afternoon he was so ill that the school asked us to come and take him home. He was examined at the hospital where we were told that no other cause was found for his sickness, like appendicitis or anything – so it must have been food poisoning – the sort that comes on very quickly.'

'Possibly,' said Mr Ponsonby, running a long elegant finger down his long elegant nose, 'but we have not got a case unless we have much more definite proof, or else we shall be laughed out of court – and that, Mr Broadbent, is something which I am not prepared to risk.'

'Well then, what happens next?'

'There are various lines of enquiry I can pursue, both at the school and at the hospital. Are you sure that you want to proceed with the case, as there will be considerable preliminary costs involved and after all, it seems that your son will make a complete recovery.'

'My son is still in a very frail state and I feel that this unfortunate episode will affect his work for the rest of the term and possibly for the whole of this school year. I think that I have every right to demand compensation.'

Geoffrey glared defiantly at the impassive Mr Ponsonby, who then stood up at his desk in a gesture of dismissal.

'Very well, Mr Broadbent, I shall make further enquiries and will contact you again as soon as is feasible.'

Three weeks later the contact came in the form of a letter. Linda handed it to her husband whilst they were having breakfast.

'This seems to be the only proper letter,' she said, 'all the rest is junk mail – oh no, here is a postcard from cousin Louise. She and Ed are in Scotland.'

But Geoffrey wasn't listening. He was tearing open the letter from Stemson, Muncaster & Ponsonby. He read it in silence and then let out a roar of anger.

'The solicitor refuses to take up our case! Says that he has carried out further investigations and we have nothing to stand on. No proof that Marcus had food poisoning. No other cases at the school. Nothing found to be the matter with the food. All the kitchen staff questioned, etc. Hospital and GP say probably a twenty-four hour stomach bug. Tests negative – blah blah blah. And he has sent me a dirty great bill for his miserable efforts – and all for nothing – *nothing*!'

Linda sat listening to his tirade and then said calmly, Geoffrey, I can't help saying that you have brought this on yourself. I never felt that trying to sue was the right thing to do and asked you not to – but all you could see was the possibility of a pot of gold at the end of it and went crashing on – it was sheer avarice – and now you have lost face. It has been no good for Marcus, no good for our relationship with the school and certainly no good for your bank balance.'

Geoffrey, who knew his wife was right, silently picked up the letter and walked out of the kitchen.

* * * * *

The following Saturday Kate was at her parent's house again. The atmosphere was very gloomy. The conversation at lunch seemed to centre alternatively around Amanda and Jake's marriage and the ridiculous amount of money that solicitors earned. After the lunch had been cleared away and the washing up done Kate felt like a breath of fresh air.

At least Marcus was physically better, but Kate could see that he was in a very depressed and worried state.

'Come on, Marky!' she said to her brother who was settling down on the settee to watch football on the television, 'a walk in the park would be a good idea.'

Marcus, who never thought a walk anywhere was a good idea was not enthusiastic.

'Why? – Doesn't sound a very good idea to me.'

'Well it is – come and keep me company – its hardly party time here, and anyway, I want a chat with you.'

A walk and a chat with your sister in the park on a Saturday afternoon did not strike Marcus as a particularly cool thing to do, but nevertheless he reluctantly extricated himself from the settee, shovelled himself into an anorak and trudged off with Kate.

It was early autumn and already leaves were swirling on the grass. Marcus kicked at them disconsolately.

'Marky,' began Kate gently, 'what's wrong?'

'Nothing, why?'

'Because I think there is something wrong.'

'Why?'

'Because I know you well enough, that's why. Something's on your mind isn't it?'

Marcus grunted and continued to kick at the leaves as if he had something against them.

But he said nothing.

'Are you still upset about the food poisoning episode?'

'Sort of.' Marcus was giving way.

'You didn't have food poisoning did you?'

'No.'

'What happened Marky? You can tell me.'

'Yeah – I think I'd feel better if I told someone and I'd rather tell you than anyone else – but promise you won't split on me?'

'Of course I promise.'

'Well, that lunchtime me and some of my mates had a Mars Bar competition.'

'What's that?'

'To see who could eat the most Mars Bars of course. We'd saved up our pocket money to buy them and we didn't even go into lunch that day.'

'And where does this orgy of gluttony take place?'

'In a corner of the school field behind the bike sheds.'

'And who won?'

'I did.'

'How many Mars Bars?'

'Seventeen.'

'No wonder you were sick!'

' I shall never be able to eat another Mars Bar again,' Marcus said with considerable fierce regret. You won't tell Dad, will you? I was going to explain it all, but then I felt so rotten and put it off and then it all got out of hand, with Dad rushing off to the school like that, and wanting to sue and stuff and then he got a bill to pay to the solicitor. I feel so bad about it Sis, but I'm too scared to tell him now. I feel better now I've told you,' he added, a little sheepishly.

Kate put an arm round her erring brother. 'We all make mistakes, Marky and we all suffer from them. And learn from them too,' she said feelingly. 'This wretched business will blow over and Dad will get over it and then, later on you will probably be able to confess about it and feel better. In fact, in time to come we shall all probably be able to laugh about it – and you can explain to your children why you never eat Mars Bars!'

Marcus grinned. 'Thanks, Sis. You're a bit of a star!'

He then saw a few of his mates kicking a football around. 'There's Chas and Mick and Co – Ok if I join them?'

'Yes, that's fine!' said Kate, pleased to see him in better spirits. 'I'll go to the other side of the park and go to the off-licence – I think we could do with a bottle of wine with supper. See you back at home later.'

Marcus went off to join his friends and Kate fastened her coat up against the increasing chill of the late afternoon. As she hurried along a path through the park she became aware of footsteps behind her. She quickened her pace but so did the person following.

Then suddenly a hefty youth was upon her, pushing her and grabbing at her shoulder bag.

'Get off!' she screamed at the top of her voice, kicking out at her assailant in fright and rage. But his strength was much superior to hers and he knocked her to the ground, where she still struggled as hard as she could, holding onto her bag as tightly as possible, still screaming, but he managed to prise her grip away from it and started to run off.

Then a snarling, powerful bundle of fury leapt upon him. This unexpected and forceful attack frightened him witless. His jacket was gripped and shaken until it tore. He made a futile attempt to lash out with the bag but his priority was to escape from the situation as quickly as possible.

'Bloody dog!' he yelled, 'get it off me!'

The dog was Bess.

'Give me my bag, you rotten thief!' Kate shouted, struggling to her feet. The youth started to run away again with Bess chasing him, barking and snapping until he threw the bag down and ran out through a gate.

'Bess, Bess!' called Kate. And Bess, clearly feeling that she had dealt satisfactorily with the unwanted company, came running back to Kate, with the bag in her mouth and her tail wagging furiously.

'Oh Bess – thank you – what a good girl!' whispered Kate in relief, and for the first time accepted the wet licks all over her face in the spirit in which they were given, as she hugged the dog with hands that had started to shake from shock.

'Here Bess, here!' shouted a voice she knew so well and Peter came running round a corner. Bess did not know whether to stay guarding Kate and carry on licking her face or leap up to her master, so she tried to do both at the same time.

'Oh Kate! It's _you_! What happened? Are you all right?'

'Yes, Bess really saved me – and my bag. She was just wonderful!' panted Kate as tears of relief began to flow. 'Oh

Peter, Peter!' Peter put his arms around her and led her to a nearby seat.

'Let's just sit here for a bit while you get your breath back.' he said gently, 'Sit, Bess – you've been such a good girl!'

Bess thumped her tail and obediently sat down, leaning heavily against them. Kate sobbed out her story, 'Some chap pounced on me and snatched my bag and Bess flew at him and then chased him off. And he dropped my bag. Bess knew me, I'm sure!'

'Of course she knew you and I'm sure that she misses you. And I miss you more than she does. How lucky that I just happened to be visiting some friends here today and I was giving Bess a run in the park.'

Kate smiled. 'Very lucky,' she whispered, as Peter took her dirty grazed face in his hands and kissed it tenderly.

* * * * *

About a month later Amanda and Kate were having a cappuccino at their usual café.

'So you and Peter are back together again?' said Amanda, smiling.

'Yes, and this time its all going to be fine. How are things between you and Jake?'

'Better. That week away we had when Mum and Dad looked after the children was great. It was wonderful having so much time just to ourselves and we really *talked* Kate. We have both been in the wrong and I think that we understand why – so we are making a new start. Madeline isn't working in the office anymore. Apparently she had her problems too. Her husband had lost his job and he had gone to live with his sister. Jake says that he has another job now and I think that they are sorting themselves out again as well. And Mike's wife Janet is going to be their new secretary – at least for the time being!'

'That's good,' said Kate, biting into her extravagant cream bun, 'that's all very good. Have you seen Mum and Dad this week?'

'No, I'm going tomorrow.'

'Give them my love – Marcus seems fine and I think he has lost a bit of weight – which can't be a bad thing. I hope that Dad is getting over all the silly and unfortunate business with the solicitor.'

'Oh, I expect he will – sooner or later. Mum reckons that he has learnt a bit of a lesson.'

'I think,' said Kate softly,' that we have all learnt a bit of a lesson lately – and mostly the hard way. And now things seem to have come around full circle!'

'There's nothing quite so effective as the hard way to *really* learn a lesson,' said Amanda,' – and a bit more about yourself! Let's have another cup of coffee!'

14 ~ An Easter Egg and a Cat's Tail

Reginald had a feeling of satisfaction as he drove his Mercedes from the town centre to his home in a leafy suburb. It was the day before the Easter holiday weekend and he had managed to leave the office early, enabling him to miss the rush hour traffic and be home in good time. This would please Penelope as they were going to a dinner party at the Martin-Johnson's that evening. Not that he was all that keen on the Martin- Johnson's – rather irritating social climbers, he thought – but Penelope had been pleased to receive the invitation. Social climbing was slightly higher on Penelope's list of priorities than he felt was strictly necessary.

Musing about the other activities they had planned for the nice long weekend, it suddenly came to him that he had forgotten all about buying an Easter egg for Penelope!

He winced as he remembered that he had made the very same omission last year and a rather unnecessary fuss had ensued. Soon, he knew, he would be passing a group of shops and he would be able to remedy the situation. What a good thing that he had remembered that he had forgotten, in time!

He soon came to a cluster of shops and slid his car into a parking space in the service road that had just conveniently been vacated by a large red van. He bounded into a newsagents and confectionary shop. As he waited to be served he watched a small black and white cat peering dramatically underneath a low shelf, willing a dry leaf which had blown in from the pavement to be a mouse. He purchased the largest beribboned Easter egg the shop had to offer and then, congratulating himself for thinking of it at the last minute, he bought a large box of chocolate drops for Marlene the Afghan hound.

Clutching his purchases in one hand and carrying his briefcase in the other, he turned to go out of the shop. As he did so he accidentally trod on the end of the twitching tail of the black and white cat. The cat let out the most almighty high-pitched howl, to the obvious alarm of everyone within earshot, and dashed out into the street. Reginald gave an embarrassed apology to anyone who was interested to listen, and hurriedly followed suit.

The cat had jumped up onto a nearby brick wall and from its safe height was crossly swishing its tail to and fro. This excited a small terrier dog who was impatiently waiting for its mistress to stop talking to someone she had met and get on with their walk to the park. The dog suddenly darted towards the wall in a vain attempt to reach the cat, pulling its lead out to its full extent just as Reginald emerged from the shop, tripped over it and went sprawling onto the pavement. The owner of the dog was most upset and profusely apologetic. The dog continued to bark excitedly at the cat and the cat, from the safety of the wall viewed the situation with feline impassiveness. Reginald managed to save the Easter egg from damage, but the box of chocolate drops fell out of his hand and disgorged some of its contents onto the pavement. The dog, realizing its efforts to reach the cat were futile, turned its attention even more excitedly to this sudden manna from heaven. Reginald picked himself up and grabbed the box from the dog which, not wanting to lose such a prize, promptly bit his finger. The dog's owner, who had been trying in vain to control her charge. was put into an overdrive of concern.

'Monty! You naughty, naughty dog!' she scolded, and turning an anxious face to Reginald effervesced with apologies. 'I'm so sorry! Oh dear, Oh dear, Monty never usually bites. Is your finger bleeding? Oh yes, it is! This is quite dreadful! Look Monty, what you have done! Naughty! Naughty! Naughty! Now we must put some antiseptic and a dressing on that finger straight away. We don't want it to go septic do we?'

A thought was flashing through Reginald's mind that a septic finger would perhaps be slightly preferable to being an object of all this fuss and bother, and that wrapping his handkerchief round the finger in question was quite adequate. But despite his protestations he found himself propelled into a nearby chemist shop. The recalcitrant dog was tied to a post outside and its owner bustled up to the pharmacy counter demanding antiseptic, dressings and immediate attention.

'This is not a major emergency,' explained an embarrassed Reginald to the assistant, 'just a packet of plasters will be fine.' Then he turned to the owner of the dog, saying, 'Thank you very much for your concern, madam, your little dog was just excited about eating our Afghan hounds chocolate drops. No real harm done. My finger will be quite all right.'

He received a beaming smile, as from one dog lover to another.

'Are you sure? Quite sure? Very well then,' and muttering 'Naughty Monty! Naughty Monty!' a few more times, she turned and hurried off, colliding with a tall man in dark glasses standing behind a carousel of hair accessories and knocking his briefcase out of his hand.

Reginald dutifully put a plaster on his finger and with relief left the shop and clambered back into his car. He put the briefcase, the Easter egg and what remained of Marlene's chocolate drops on the back seat. After his unscheduled delay he found that the traffic had built up somewhat and he was soon waiting in a queue at some traffic lights. He was behind a carpet layer's van which had rolls of carpet and vinyl poking out at the back of it. The rear door handles were rather inadequately tied together with string, and when the van jerked into a start when the lights changed, the string gave way and several of the rolls fell out into the path of Reginald's car. Cursing, he ploughed into them before he screeched to a stop. He furiously leapt out of his car, waving his fists at the van driver who was looking with horror at his ruined merchandise and the damaged bumper and offside light of the depressingly expensive-looking car behind him.

'What the hell do you think you're playing at, driving along like that?' Reginald was shouting.

'If you hadn't been so bloody close you could've stopped in time!'

'Rubbish – you were driving with a dangerous load! And look what you've done to my car!'

Soon, amidst hooting and honking, the other traffic came to a halt and a crowd of onlookers began to gather. How people delight in viewing other's misfortunes!

Then two policemen arrived on the scene to investigate the commotion – two angry men, one damaged Mercedes, rolls of carpet and vinyl obstructing the road and traffic at an impatient standstill.

When the road had been cleared and in single file, the traffic moved on, the policemen questioned Reginald and the driver of the van in more detail. The van driver was belligerent and Reginald full of righteous anger and indignation.

'May I see your driving licence, Sir?' one of the policeman asked Reginald, in the polite but firm and somewhat disapproving voice that the arm of the law use on such occasions.

'Certainly, I have it in my briefcase,' Reginald scowled, resenting being treated as if he were a criminal. He reached into his car and took out the briefcase from the back seat – but although it was very similar to his there was something unfamiliar about it. It wasn't his briefcase! With the policeman standing over him he snapped it open. It was brim full of bundles of bank notes!

'Well, well, WELL!' almost gloated the policeman, at the realisation that this traffic incident was turning out to be more interesting than he could have hoped, 'What have we here?'

Reginald was staring at the contents of the briefcase in amazement and horror. His mouth suddenly became dust dry and momentarily he was speechless.

'B-b-but this is not my briefcase!' he managed to squeak, in a voice hardly recognisable as his own.

'Oh no?' said the policeman, sounding unconvinced. 'I think, Sir, you had better come back to the station with me – we are currently investigating the theft of a large number of banknotes.'

Reginald felt outraged, frustrated and bewildered and realised that he had no option other than to resign himself to be taken, for the first time in his life, to a police station.

'What about my car?' he managed to query.

'You come with me and my colleague will drive your car – which looks perfectly drivable, to the station when he has finished dealing with the other gentleman. I will take the briefcase, thank you.' And with that he bundled Reginald into the police car – much to the increased interest of the spectators.

In his misery Reginald hoped that there was nobody who knew or recognised him. And what about Penelope? Whatever was she going to say to all this? Perhaps he ought to have a blanket over his head, like criminals one sees on the television? But no such option was provided.

At the police station various formalities were gone through and then he was taken into a room for questioning. He felt that this must be all a bad dream and that soon he would, with relief, wake from it.

An investigating officer settled himself in a chair opposite to Reginald.

Now, Mr – er Fitzwilliam,' he said,' before we commence, would you like to make a telephone call?'

'Yes, I would like to phone my wife.'

Soon he heard Penelope's shrill voice at the other end of the phone. 'Reginald! Where are you? I rang your mobile and some awful man answered, said something very rude which I can't possibly repeat, and cut off! Reginald, I'm so worried. Are you all right? Shall I contact the police?'

'There is no need to do that, as I happen at the moment, to be at a police station.'

The phone crackled wildly at this. 'At a police station! Whatever for! Oh Reginald, how terrible!'

'Penelope, just calm down. There has been a misunderstanding, which I'm sure will be sorted out. I'll give you a ring later.'

'But what sort of misunderstanding? And what about the dinner party tonight at the Martin-Johnson's?'

'You will have to say that we can't come.'

'What? Tell them you can't come because you are practically in prison?'

'No, don't be silly, think of another reason – even if I do get home in time, which I doubt, about the last thing I would want to do is to go to dinner with the Martin-Johnsons.'

'But Reginald –' Penelope was about to go into top gear.

'Look Penelope, I must go. Don't worry, everything will be all right and I'll ring you again as soon as I can.'

With that Reginald put the phone down and looked resignedly at the investigating officer in front of him.

'Sorry about that – but my wife is in a bit of a fret.'

'I can understand that,' the officer replied, 'but now I have quite few questions to ask you.'

Reginald was feeling calmer now. This man seemed perfectly reasonable and he felt that this bizarre situation would be sorted out satisfactorily.

'You say that this briefcase does not belong to you?' the officer continued, 'and if this is so, how do you think it could have come into your possession? Are you sure that you had your own brief case when you left your office?'

'Of course, and I have no idea how I came to have the briefcase with all that money in it. I wonder where the hell my briefcase is now? I had some quite important papers in it.'

'That we don't know,' was the reply. 'Did you stop anywhere, for petrol or anything after you left the office?'

'Yes – I stopped to buy an Easter egg.'

And then everything was pieced together – the cat, the dog, the chemist shop, the dog's owner bumping into the tall man and knocking his briefcase out of his hand – it was then that the briefcases must have become mixed up. With relief Reginald felt that he was no longer under serious suspicion.

'You see,' said the officer,' we are very actively searching for a gang who recently raided a Building Society and got away with a large amount of money. We know that they have now split up. We have caught one of them, but the others are still at large. I suppose you haven't noticed a large red tool hire van around in your travels?'

'I didn't notice what the van had written on it,' Reginald replied, ' but a red van was just leaving the service road as I arrived at the row of shops – I know that because I then went into its parking space – there were no others available.'

The officer appeared very interested about this. He pushed his chair back and stood up.

'PC Baxter here will stay with you,' he said, 'You must excuse me for a few minutes.

Would you like a cup of tea? I could ask for one to be brought in?'

Reginald said yes, he would like a cup of tea.

And then he had another cup of tea.

After that he was asked to wait in different room, where he sat listening to all the off-stage noises emanating from around him – doors banging, people shouting, hurrying footsteps, telephones, protestations – what a way, he thought, to start the holiday weekend! He thought about Penelope wondering what was happening to him. He would phone her again as soon as he could – or as soon as he had something positive to say.

Then he heard quite a commotion going on. There was a lot of scuffling and the sounds of a struggle. A dog was barking and men were shouting.

Eventually the investigating officer who had interviewed him earlier came in the room, looking very cheerful indeed.

'We've got him – the man you exchanged briefcases with! He was lying low in the corner of the amenity tip not far from those shops you went into. The dog sniffed him out – and then we found your briefcase in one of the skips. It looks a bit the worse for wear, but as it is locked, presumably all your papers are still in it.

You are perfectly free to go – with apologies for all the inconvenience and thanks for your help.'

With relief Reginald took his briefcase, shook the officer's hand and in no time was almost skipping down the police station steps. But his day was not over yet – in his haste he missed a step, lost his balance and for the second time that day he fell. He felt a bang on his head, as if from another world where everything was blackness.

* * * * *

When he came back into his own world he found himself in a hospital bed. He closed his eyes again against the hammering pain in his head. The next time he opened them he had a blurred vision of an anxious Penelope bending over him.

'Reginald! Reginald! Speak to me! Are you all right?

'I don't know. Probably not.'

'My poor darling.'

His vision became a little clearer. 'I've got the mother and father of a headache. What's all this stuff doing on my head?'

'It's a dressing, because you fell and cut your head and now it seems to be going a funny colour. They said that you got bad concussion but you'd be all right if you came round and started to talk.'

'Oh, good.'

'Oh Reginald – what ever happened? Whatever have you been doing?'

'All I was doing, my little sugar plum fairy, was buying you an Easter egg.

'Happy Easter!'

And with that Reginald closed his eyes again.

15 ~ A Slight Contingency

Edwina's car squealed in protest as she swerved it into the car park at Brussels airport. The suffering vehicle jerked to a halt.

'Here we are, Mother,' Edwina stated unnecessarily, drawing her long legs out of the car. 'I'll go and get a trolley.'

'Thank you dear,' said Marion. She watched her daughter-in-law stride off with intent.

She gave a small sigh. Edwina, she thought, was very admirable, but she felt that they were on somewhat different wavelengths.

'Right,' announced Edwina, returning triumphant with trolley. 'I'll come and make sure that you check in OK.'

'You needn't do that dear, – I'll be perfectly all right.'

Marion doubted very much if Edwina believed this, but felt compelled to say it just the same. Edwina steered her to the appropriate check-in desk and tut-tutted at the length of the queue.

'I'll get you a magazine for the plane,' she said. 'Make sure you don't lose your place in the queue.'

Marion smiled resignedly and began to study the usual diverse collection of people encountered at any airport. There were laughing, noisy backpackers, middle-aged holidaymakers with too much luggage, couples compulsively embracing, families with fretful children, students in their uniform of worn out jeans and trainers and businessmen with briefcases. There were tourists from North, South, East and West, including a party of orthodox Jews resplendent in long flowing coats and wonderfully huge black hats. Some people were fussing, others looking aloof with a 'I-have-done-this-so-many-times-before' expression – like the tall man standing next to Marion. He was of indeterminate race and dressed in what could be described as smart casuals. He smiled down at her in a tolerant slightly patronising manner. It was at times like these that Marion wished that she were at least six feet tall instead of five feet nothing.

Edwina appeared, clutching a glossy magazine with a picture of an English country garden on the front cover.

'This was about the most sensible magazine I could find,' she panted. 'Some of them are quite dreadful, like *The New Look City Girl, The Peekaboo Magazine,* and *Woman Wonderful.* Imagine it! I can't think what trash is in them. Most unsuitable. Anyway, I think that this one has some nice recipes in it.'

'Thank you, dear,' said Marion, taking her sensible magazine, 'I'm sure I shall enjoy it.'

'Now, you are sure that Anne is meeting you at Heathrow? Does she know your flight number and which terminal you are arriving at?'

'Yes, I know that Anne will be there. Anyway, I have my mobile phone.'

'What a good job Simon insisted you had one. I hope you can use it OK? In any case, I'll phone Anne when I get home to make sure that she has the time right. The plane may land early – or it may be delayed.'

'Edwina dear, I don't think it is necessary to phone Anne. If I arrive at the airport before her, I shall wait until she comes and if the plane is late she will wait until I appear. Now please stop worrying about it.'

'Oh very well, but I do like to think ahead in case there are *contingencies.'*

'It's very difficult to plan for contingencies, because they come in all shapes and sizes and as the only thing to do is to cope with them as best as you can if or when they arise,' answered Marion calmly.

Before Edwina could answer, it seemed that the tall man behind Marion was pushed forward. He dropped the bag he was holding, his ticket and other papers scattered to the floor and he proceeded to retrieve them. Marion was just about to offer to help him when the quickness of his hand did not quite deceive her sharp eye. She was sure that he had deftly slipped something into the zipped compartment of her case. Her instinct was to protest immediately – but in seconds, thoughts flashed through her mind which prevented her. It was her turn at the check-in and Edwina, who had noticed nothing, grabbed her case and put it on the moving platform to be weighed. As it wobbled out of sight Marion looked for and saw, a tiny bulge in the soft-topped side pocket.

'It's been so good to have been with you and Simon and the children', Marion said as she and Edwina approached passport control. 'Thank you for such a nice time.'

'You must come again soon, when we can arrange it and if you feel that you can manage the journey, as we're here for another two years.'

'Yes, I know – that would be lovely.' Marion said, and added, before Edwina could ask her, 'now I have my passport and my ticket and my boarding card – so goodbye dear – my love to you all, and thank you again.'

They kissed each other and Edwina hurried away, waving as Marion smilingly gave her passport to the waiting official.

She found a convenient seat in the departure lounge from where she had a good view of the information screen and her fellow travellers arriving and settling down to await boarding instructions. She hardly stood out in the crowd – small, conventional, grey-haired and flat- shoed. She assumed that, for this very reason, the tall stranger had targeted her to plant something illicit in her luggage in order to smuggle it through customs. Of course, she could be entirely wrong – her imagination had always tended to run away with her. However, in case her suspicions were correct, she must think out a course of action.

With her various items of hand luggage gathered around her, she sat and watched. Soon she saw him. The tall man. She looked away so that she could see him only from the corner of her eye. Was he looking for her? He sauntered nonchalantly in her direction and settled in a seat some way away from her. She was aware that he gave her just a fleeting glance. She studied the information screen, looked at her watch and opened her newspaper.

She could not help sensing a ridiculous little thrill that she knew, or thought she knew, something that he didn't think she knew. That thought, however, was tempered by her wondering what his plan may be when they reached Heathrow.

She boarded the plane before the tall man. She sank insignificantly into her seat by the window and watched him settle on the other side of the plane a little in front of her. Fairly soon they were up and away. Brussels diminished and disappeared. Gazing out of the window as they soared above the amazing clouds, she thought hard and decided what she would do – just in case her suspicions were correct.

Then she tried to relax. She opened Edwina's sensible magazine and leafed through it, knowing full well that she would cook none of the recipes it gave or subject her garden to any of the time-consuming activities that were suggested.

The flight proceeded uneventfully. Every now and then she stared at the back of the tall man's head. Not once did she notice him turn and look at her. What if her imagination *had* been running riot?

The pilot's voice floated out of the speakers, informing his passengers that they were now approaching Heathrow, the weather was mild and wet and he hoped everyone had enjoyed the flight. Marion's heart began to beat faster as she obediently fastened her seat belt. The unfathomable technology of flight never ceased to amaze her, but on this occasion this was not the only factor causing her heart to thump so. She felt the engines reversing and reigning in the plane's speed as the runway rose to meet it.

The landing was smooth – and then the stillness of the plane was counteracted by the surge of activity inside it. To a crescendo of voices everyone was collecting possessions together, slamming overhead locker doors, shovelling themselves into coats and anoraks and queuing in the aisles to alight. The steps were wheeled out, the door opened and the passengers single-filed out onto terra firma. The tall man was in front of Marion.

Walking across the tarmac he put his travel bag down and adjusted the fastenings of his coat until she went past him. Now he was walking quite close behind her.

The baggage collection area was seething with people. This was in her favour. If she was in danger it would not be until she had come through Customs. What she needed was time – and a Ladies.

Ensconced in a cubicle she fumbled her mobile phone out of her handbag.

'Anne?'

'Mum! I wondered if you'd ring my mobile. Where are you?'

'In a Ladies in baggage – can't talk very loudly. Are you in Arrivals yet? Can you hear me?'

'Yes to both.'

'There's a complication. Listen carefully and do just what I say.'

'Mum?'

Marion explained as much as she felt she needed to, feeling grateful that her daughter was very level headed.

'Oh Mum, be careful! I'll ring you back shortly.'

Marion emerged from the Ladies and joined the bunches of people waiting for their luggage to appear from the darkness and bumble around the carousel. The tall man she felt, had been waiting for her, although feigning complete disinterest in her. He wandered away from the crowd to use his mobile phone. The ubiquitous mobile phone, mused Marion, certainly has its uses! His conversation was brief and he then placed himself a discreet distance from her by the carousel. There was a satisfactory wait before her familiar case came circling around. She retrieved it, feeling reunited with an old friend. The slight bulge in the pocket was still there. Finding a trolley, she took as long as possible arranging her possessions upon it, placing the case one way and then another. She then fussed about checking in her handbag for her passport and her purse and her handkerchief. All the time she was acutely conscious of the tall man aloofly hovering in the background. Then her mobile phone rang from the depths of her handbag.

Anne's voice crackled, 'Mum, it should be OK. – and someone will keep an eye on you between Customs and Arrivals. Take care!'

Marion spoke loudly and cheerfully into her phone for the benefit of her listener. ' Yes, I'm just leaving the baggage hall. Yes, lovely time. See you soon!'

She trundled her trolley sedately along towards Customs. She sensed that the tall man was quite close behind her now. Passing through 'Nothing to Declare' an official appeared, which was comforting, as this was the time she knew she would feel vulnerable. And there was Anne, with an expression hovering between anxiety and relief, waiting at the barrier. Close to her were two satisfactorily substantial men in casual clothes. Mother and daughter hugged each other and then pushed the trolley away from the greeting crowd.

'The tall man – a bit behind,' whispered Marion softly, – 'we'll have to give him a chance to grab the case.'

'Police are nice and handy,' Anne whispered reassuringly in reply.

When the crowd thinned a little, they stopped pushing the trolley and slightly turning their backs on it, became involved in looking at a map of Brussels which Marion produced from her handbag. Sure enough, the tall man walked past, swiftly picked up the case and disappeared into the crowd. All according to plan – so far!

Shortly there was a lot of shouting and scuffling near to the exit signs. Marion and Anne hurried to see what was going on. There were policemen, security guards, customs officers and flashing cameras – and in the centre of the mayhem three struggling, handcuffed men were being led away. One was the tall man who, on seeing Marion in the crowd, gave her an especially unpleasant snarl.

* * * * *

The diamonds, sealed in a neat package, lay in tiny pockets in a length of soft velvety material. They were worth a great deal of money.

'Ladies!' the senior customs officer said to Marion and Anne when they were in his office drinking a welcome cup of tea, 'We are extremely grateful to you – we have been after this gang for some time – and we've caught three of them red handed – the tall man who was on the 'plane and his two accomplices waiting here. We have been working with officials from Amsterdam, Antwerp and Brussels – and your pluck and good sense have been invaluable!'

'Excellent!' said Marion, 'One must always be prepared to cope with contingencies! Thank you so much for the tea. Is it all right for us to go home now? Who, by the way, are all those people outside?'

'That's the press – they are always here waiting for celebrities or a good story – you'll be in the papers tomorrow!'

Later, at home in Marion's cottage, Anne said laughing, 'can you imagine how surprised Edwina is going to be when she reads in the paper – 'GRANDMOTHER FOILS DIAMOND SMUGGLERS?'

'Not quite as surprised as she would be if she knew that I have just received this letter from *Women Wonderful* magazine, saying that they liked the items I sent them and could I write some more?!'

16 ~ The Christmas Shoppers

The departmental store is seething horribly with Christmas shoppers. The Christmas shoppers are festooned with parcels and bags and it seems that every other female is either manoeuvring a buggy through the throng or is accompanied by a fretful toddler.

Over the terrible tinkling noise emanating from a mechanical Father Christmas ringing a festive bell Charles hears his wife's voice.

'Charles! Charles, – I'm over here, – in Scarves and Gloves. Now do you think that Auntie Maureen would like this purple scarf?'

'If she likes purple scarves and she hasn't got ten already she might.'

'Charles, that's not very helpful.'

'I'm not good at helpful Christmas shopping.'

'Why did you come then?'

'Because you absolutely insisted that I did.'

'Well now you are here perhaps we could choose some presents together?'

'All right then, lets get the purple scarf for Auntie Maureen.'

'I'm not sure about it now – you've put me off it a bit. We'll just keep it in mind and go and look for something for Uncle Bert. What do you think he'd like?'

'Probably to be left in peace to mess about in his potting shed all over Christmas – preferably with one or two bottles of wine.'

'Well he won't get much chance to do that – Auntie Maureen is having all the family to stay for the whole holiday.'

'Poor Bert – perhaps we could buy him an outfit to be Father Christmas in?'

'That's a silly suggestion, Charles – I think I'll buy him some socks.'

'That will probably make him sick with excitement – you wouldn't want that.'

'I'll pretend I didn't hear that. We can get a pair of these and a pair of these. Where do we pay? I can't see, its all so crowded.'

'Over there – I'll go.'

'Thank you dear, – I'll see you in Toys and Games – we must get the presents for the children.'

Some time later husband and wife are reunited amongst a sea of bright coloured plastic – a good proportion of which was capable of flashing lights and emitting squeaks and whirrs or disembodied American voices.

'Here you are Janet, thought I'd never find you. Have you got all the toys?'

'Of course not. It takes ages to choose them. We'll start with Linda's baby – he must be about eight months now.'

'What do babies of eight months do?'

'They crawl about and put things in their mouths and rattle things and shake things – that sort of thing.'

'So we are looking for something that he can put in his mouth and preferably rattle and shake at the same time, whilst crawling?'

'Not necessarily. Oh! – here is a sweet little blue cuddly rabbit – let's get him this!'

'Won't he choke on it?'

'No. Now there's Sally – what for her?'

'Here's a skipping rope – she needs to get off the sofa and lose a bit of weight.'

'What if she doesn't like skipping?'

'Let's get it anyway.'

'Oh, all right – I'll say you chose it. Now let me find my list. Mmm – children – Claire, Annie, Michael, Andrew, Clarissa, Marcus, Alexander and William.'

'All those?'

'I know that Marcus wants one of those robots with red flashing eyes.'

'That's enough to give him nightmares.'

'Never mind, that's what he wants – Jennifer says. Then we'll go and look at the puzzles and games and the dolls. I'm sure that Claire would like a Barbie doll.'

'What's a Barbie doll?'

'It's a grown up doll with different outfits and handbags and things.'

'What does a little girl want a doll like that for? I thought that dolls were supposed to be babies. My sister's dolls were her pretend babies.'

'You're out of date, Charles. Dolls, like everything else have changed. Don't worry about it. There they are – next isle along.'

'They're awful – all stiff and sexy. How will Claire feel maternal about a doll like that?'

'Girls aren't supposed to feel maternal these days – its all to do with sexual equality. Anyway, never mind that – let's have this one all dressed up to go to a party.'

'Well, has she got her handbag?'

'Of course.'

'Just checking.'

'Perhaps we can get games and books for the others – they are nice and easy to wrap up.'

After suitable deliberations seemingly interminable to Charles, a collection of games and books are selected and Charles and Janet leave the toy department carrying bulging plastic bags decorated with beaming Father Christmases surrounded by festive stars.

There seems to be more determined shoppers than ever swarming about the store now – some grim-faced and some even cheerful. A number of children are screaming their heads off, others miraculously sleeping in their buggies, blissfully oblivious of the trauma of the Christmas season and others tearing around completely out of control of their harassed parents. Electronic tills squeak and squawk and seasonal music blares from the sound system. Husbands wait disconsolately outside changing rooms and grandmothers rest aching feet if they are fortunate enough to find an empty chair.

Charles has a happy thought. 'Janet, – I think that our parking time will be running out – we had better go now or we may get a parking ticket.'

'Oh, Charles, be a darling and go and put some more money in the meter – there are a few more things that we really must try and get now we're here. I'll see you in Lingerie – I want to choose a nightie for Mother and …'

But Charles does not wait to hear about the delights the lingerie department has to offer and with a sigh of resignation pushes his way through the crowd with the first contingent of parcels to find his way back to the car park.

After some time husband and wife are reunited, amongst a froth of nightwear. It has to be decided which night attire would be nicest for Mother.

'What about this one with these pretty little pink bows round the neck, Charles?'

'Lovely.'

'Or this blue one?'

'Lovely.'

'I think I'll get the pink one – Mother likes pink – and while we're here we can get a petticoat for Mabel and a bed jacket for Dawn so that she can take it into hospital when she goes – if ever she gets to the top of the waiting list.'

'How far down is she?'

'Fairly at the bottom I think.'

'Let's hope that she doesn't wear the bed jacket out beforehand then.'

'Don't be so cynical, Charles.

'I think it's all this Christmas shopping that's making me cynical.'

'That's ridiculous, it's a very happy thing to do.'

'These three Madam?' interrupts the assistant.

'Yes please – just let me check that I have the right sizes.'

More parcels join their already burdened arms and more gifts are pondered over and bought or rejected or almost bought and then changed at the last minute.

As Charles is fearing for his bank balance Janet says, 'Now, Charles, what about our presents for each other? It would be quite fun choosing them now, together wouldn't it? We have got beyond the stage of having to have surprises.'

Charles is led to the handbag and luggage department. 'I really would like a new handbag dear. Everyone has black handbags these days and my black one has got very tatty. Oh look here's some black ones – lots. I said black bags are in – there are hardly any coloured ones at all.'

'You choose one then – Happy Christmas!'

'Oh thank you darling – which one do you like?'

'I don't know what sort you want – you just go ahead and choose.'

The choice takes a long time, but is eventually made and the lady duly pleased.

'I would like to buy you a shirt dear – you could certainly do with a new one – lets find the men's department. I think its downstairs.'

Downstairs they go where they are confronted with what seems like an acre of male clothing and the shirts are located.

'Oh Charles, how about this mauve one – that would be a change for you.'

'It certainly would, because I hate mauve.'

'Pity. How about this one, or this, or this?'

'I don't like any of those, I just want a plain blue shirt.'

'Very well, but its rather dull of you. Here are some – make sure they have your size.'

'Yes they have, this is fine – lets get to the pay desk while it doesn't look too busy.'

'Oh Charles – I think that my account must be getting rather low – could you possibly do it on yours?'

At last they are in the car and queuing up to get out of the multi-storey.

At last they are at home.

Shoeless, Janet is flopped in an armchair with a cup of tea. 'Well, that was a really lovely shopping outing wasn't it?'

Charles is pouring himself a whisky.

'You could say that, but I cannot possibly comment.'

17 ~ A Love Affair

Once more that night the distressed cry had roused her from a shallow sleep. She was programmed to respond, and did so instantly. She slipped into the waiting dressing gown and hurried into the adjoining room. Making crooning, comforting noises, she let down the side of the cot and momentarily the crying ceased. Two thin arms were held feebly up to her, and lovingly, gently, she lifted the baby and held him closely to her.

'There, there, Joe Brown Eyes – Mummy's here – its all right now.'

She sat in the low nursery chair and rocked him to and fro, kissing him over and over, as if to kiss away the fever and the laboured breathing. The child responded to her touch and her voice. The tensed body relaxed and the large brown eyes, which seemed to take up a disproportionate share of space in the small thin face, closed, opened and then closed again.

She continued rocking her baby, gazing at him and humming softly. Her mind went back to the time when after six years of wanting a baby, her pregnancy was confirmed. She had enjoyed the waiting time – preparing the nursery, reading the baby books, laughing with Jeff about all the things that they would do when they were a family and so looking forward to having a child to love and look after.

The baby had arrived earlier than expected. It was not a straightforward delivery – but at last – there he was, a baby boy – how wonderful! She had closed her eyes, waiting to hear that first welcome cry. It was rather a long time before it came – but yes, there it was! Her baby was fine!

The midwife had put him in her arms. 'He's beautiful!' she had said to Jeff happily, and they rejoiced together.

Shortly afterwards a doctor had come to examine the baby. 'Just routine,' he explained. Then the midwife said, 'we are just going to pop him into the Special Care Unit for a wee while dear – he needs a little bit of help with his breathing.' She smiled brightly. 'Don't worry – you'll see him again soon.'

That was the beginning. There were more examinations, consultations and appointments. She recalled phrases such as 'Its not very good news I'm afraid, Mr and Mrs Allen and 'rare syndrome, affecting nerves and muscles' and 'counselling, plenty of support.'

She refused to believe it all. Her baby would be all right. She loved him so much and would look after him so well that he would soon pick up and be strong and healthy. Her love was a match for any syndrome – and whoever needs counselling to look after one's own baby for goodness sake? The sooner she had him home and away from all these well-meaning professionals and their tubes and monitors and scans, the better.

Jeff was very supportive but rather quiet and thoughtful – but that was his way.

She sent her pretty announcement cards to all her family and friends, with a little note on the bottom saying that Joe was still in hospital 'having a bit of an eye kept on him' but soon he would be home. A sea of blue congratulation cards arrived and she put them up in the waiting nursery.

'Do you remember the day you came home, my darling?' she asked her Joe. It was all so exciting – and everyone thought that you were really lovely and at last I could look after you myself. There was just you and me – and Daddy, of course.'

Looking after Joe took up practically all her time. He took his feeds painfully slowly.

He cried a lot, and needed constant comforting. But she didn't mind. 'He likes me with him all the time,' she said happily to her sister on the phone, 'I'm afraid he's getting dreadfully spoilt! It's a good job that Mum can come over quite a lot and help in the house and get Jeff's supper etc. Mind you, Jeff seems to have to go away on business rather more these days.'

The Health Visitor came and said that she was looking after Joe beautifully.

'Can I come to your clinic and have Joe weighed?'

'Of course, you would be most welcome! Come and meet some of the other mothers.'

So she did. She had often noticed mothers trailing their baby buggies and toddlers to the clinic and had wistfully longed to be one of their number. Everyone at the clinic was very friendly, delighting in undiluted baby talk, whilst drinking tea and coping with hectic toddlers. They admired Joe and said what lovely big brown eyes he had.

After several further visits to the clinic however, she saw that other babies of Joe's age were smiling and cooing, holding toys and chuckling, then sitting up, then trying to crawl. They put on weight each week and some of them were as fat as butter. The most she could expect Joe to put on was 30 or 60 grams, or at least she could be pleased if he hadn't actually lost any weight. Soon she felt that it was not necessary to go to the clinic any more. In fact she didn't seem to have the time or need to go anywhere very much, apart from the local shops or round the nearby park, as Joe had come to like the rhythmic movement of his buggy. When friends asked her and Jeff to upper she declined because she wouldn't leave Joe with anyone else for very long.

'I would worry so, you see – he so often wakes, and I am the only person who can calm him.'

So she and Joe were cocooned in their own little world. She felt that all the love she had for him would somehow compensate for his inability to thrive, for his distress, for his now misshapen body and the limbs which wouldn't work properly. And he gave her so much back in return – the crooked smiles he had only for her, the recognition of her voice and her face and the delight she experienced over each tiny step of progress which she willed him into making. She eventually had to accept the fact that he had 'Special Needs.' She quite liked the word 'Special.'

Appointments to see specialists and therapists were dutifully kept. It was suggested that she and Jeff should have genetic counselling. Another appointment. They were told that there was no reason to expect that any subsequent children they may have would be affected like Joe. Jeff was very pleased about this, but she was not interested in having any more children. She could not imagine being able to love another child as much as she loved Joe. Anyway, she and Jeff hardly ever made love these days – she was too tired and in bed she was all the time half listening for Joe to wake.

Joe suddenly stirred and stiffened in her arms and weakly and hoarsely started to cry. She managed to get him to take a little drink and massaged and cooled his little body with a soft sponge. His breathing was worsening and she felt that he was possibly developing a chest infection. He had been prone to these for some time now, and at increasingly frequent intervals. She knew the drill – phone the hospital, rush him in – straight into the Special Unit. Then there would be the tubes, the needles, the drip, the oxygen, the monitor and the antibiotics. His small twisted body looked so pathetic and completely helpless in the cot and it all made him so utterly miserable and she suffered and suffered with him.

On the last occasion that he was admitted she had left his cubicle for a short time and when she came back there was a cluster of students around him.

'You don't have opportunities to see a child with this particular syndrome very often,' the consultant was saying in an undertone, but not realising that she had returned, 'they may have a first birthday, but extremely rarely a second. However, when he is brought in with an infection our policy is to treat him with antibiotics.' She felt like screaming, 'Go away! Go away! This is my baby and I love him, and he is not an exhibit or just a syndrome!'

She looked at him now and the large brown eyes stared up to her face and then closed again. What is all this treatment for? Just so that he has to go through it all over and over? He had become her whole world and she loved him too much to let him bear any more suffering. She wished that Jeff was here, but he was away again. She suddenly realised how much she needed him.

'Mummy's darling Brown Eyes,' she whispered, kissing the closed eyes as gently as a touch of thistledown, 'nothing is going to hurt you any more and I shall always, always love you.'

She did not know how long she sat there rocking him in her arms and sometimes singing to him softly. She felt his fever subside as his breathing became slower. A pale dawn light began to seep through the balloons and teddy bears on the nursery curtains. The wooden train on wheels that had never been pulled along and the stacking bricks which had never been stacked formed into shapes from shadows.

She let her tears brim and flow, dampening the soft blue blanket before she reached for the telephone.

18 ~ A Useful Facility

'He was out there digging again today!'

Silence.

'Jack, – I said he was digging again today!'

Vera's voice went into shrill mode. 'Why can't you listen to what I say?'

Jack came out of his evening paper. 'Because you say too much, too often – and occasionally I have something better to do.'

Vera made a kind of snorting noise, designed to denote half anger, half contempt – but was not going to be diverted from her theme. 'I said he was out there, digging – like he was yesterday.'

'Who, out where?'

'The man next door.' Vera twitched at the curtain.

'What, in his garden?'

'Yes, of course in his garden, stupid.'

'In his garden – digging?'

'Yes.'

'I can see the headlines in the National Press already – MAN SEEN IN HIS GARDEN – DIGGING.' Jack returned to his paper – to have it snatched out of his hands.

'You irritating man!' Vera snapped, duly letting herself be irritated. 'Can't you see – its rather *sinister*?'

'What's sinister about a man digging his own garden, woman? It may have escaped your notice, but the English are a nation of garden lovers. I have been known to dig my garden from time to time, to plant my potatoes and escape from your nagging tongue.'

Vera's lips made a thin line as she chose to ignore his last remark. 'For one thing,' she continued dramatically, 'he is digging a hole – an *oblong hole,* and for another he has been doing it in the evenings, furtive like – sometimes when it has been almost dark, and, *and* – 'here a knowing, almost triumphant look spread over her face as she folded her arms and glared at her husband, 'I haven't seen his wife about for almost two weeks!'

Jack's mouth fell open. 'You can't mean that you think that …?'

'I didn't say that I think anything except that it is *sinister.*'

'For a person who makes it seem some sort of virtue not to 'neighbour', how do know that his wife isn't around? She hardly comes in most days to have coffee or borrow a cup of sugar – as you made it quite clear as soon as they moved in that you are not a dispenser of coffee or a lender of sugar.'

'Of course I know she's not around – there has been no washing on the line, the hoover hasn't been going in the day – I heard it once – and that was in the evening, and the living room curtains have not always been drawn back. She usually goes out shopping or whatever, at about half past ten most mornings, but I haven't seen her, as I said, for about a fortnight.'

'Then why didn't you call round to ask if she was all right? They haven't been here long We ought to ask them in for a drink or something.'

'I'm not one for poking my nose into other people's business!'

Jack let that one go and said wearily, 'I don't want to hear any more of your evil rubbishy gossip – I just want my tea.'

'I want my tea,' Vera mimicked, 'I'm fed up with running around after you, morning, noon and night. I've done it for 28 years and I've had enough!'

'You and me both,' Jack muttered under his breath as Vera stomped out into the kitchen.

The following evening when Jack came home from work Vera was twitching at the curtains in a high state of excitement. 'Paving slabs and bags of concrete were delivered today and a roll of something which looked like very thick plastic –

probably to put her in!' She spat out this information to Jack as soon as he walked in. She had only what could be described as an 'I told you so' expression on her face. 'He's out there now, mixing up the concrete – I can't see all that clearly because that apple tree is in the way.'

'Perhaps,' suggested Jack, 'you could ask him to cut it down in order that you can spy on him more easily?'

'Trust you to say something ridiculous like that. I'm only being a responsible citizen,' Vera retorted – and looking forward to her moment of glory, she said, ' When shall we tell the Police?'

Her husband intervened hastily. 'Don't you get involved with the Police,' he said firmly, 'I expect that there is a perfectly simple explanation. Tomorrow is Saturday – leave it to me.'

'Getting all masterful are we? You are bound to make a mess of the whole thing if you have anything to do with it,' Vera said sulkily.

The following morning Jack was out early, pottering in his garden. Sure enough, there was his neighbour making up a concrete mix by the side of a deep rectangular hole.

'Morning!' Jack said cheerfully.

His neighbour looked up and came up to the fence. 'I'm afraid I'm rather deaf – you'll have to speak up!'

'You look as if you've quite a job on!' Jack shouted.

'Yes, I'm building a pond – my wife has always wanted one. She's in hospital getting a new hip, and I'm hoping to have it finished by the time she comes home, as a surprise. They push people out pretty quickly these days – so it's a bit of a race against time!'

'Would you like me to give you a hand?' Jack offered eagerly.

Some help would be most welcome – how very kind. I'm Bob, by the way Bob Weston.'

'Jack Seymour. Pleased to meet you!'

Jack was soon over the fence and spading the concrete mix. Out of the corner of his eye he saw Vera looking out of the window. Involuntarily a smile spread over his face, as he imagined her reaction to this turn of events. He peered down the hole. 'It's quite deep isn't it?' he said, 'it's a wonder that you didn't get some machinery in to dig it out?'

'Couldn't get hold of a small digger and a larger one wouldn't have got into the garden. Fortunately I've a pretty strong back – and I've certainly had plenty of exercise!

I want to put some golden carp in and they need quite deep water. With your very welcome help I can get the plastic lining in shortly and when the slabs are concreted around it will be ready to be filled with water.'

'Your wife will be delighted!' shouted Jack.

Jack spent a very enjoyable time with his neighbour, the paving slabs and the satisfying squelchy concrete mix. Vera was in a near state of apoplexy when he came back to the house for lunch – which hadn't even been thought about.

'He's getting it all ready for her,' Jack said, washing his hands at the kitchen sink and grinning to himself.

Vera was almost lost for words – but only almost. 'Whatever do you think you're about?' she screeched, 'you'll be accused of being an accessory!'

'You'd better contact the Police then.' Jack challenged. 'that would read well in the local paper!'

At this, Vera was reduced, not exactly to silence, but to incoherent noises as if she were trying to dispose of a mouthful of feathers.

A few days later Jack and Vera were invited to come and view the pond, complete with water. 'Oh! A fish pond – how nice.' said Vera. There was a thinly disguised look of disappointment on her face which only Jack was aware of.

'It's a bit slippery round the edge,' warned Bob, 'so do be careful. I'm planning to have a pump installed and have some sort of simple fountain. The fish like well aerated water.'

He then invited Jack to see some of the equipment he had bought. Jack followed Bob across the lawn to the garden shed. They had almost reached the shed when only Jack heard a surprised scream and a splash. Then silence, followed by more splashing and a gurgling calling of his name. He was well aware of the fact that Vera could not swim, and falling into water brought on one of her panic attacks. He clenched his fists and steeled himself not to look round. The splashings and gurglings lessened and then ceased. The pond became silent.

After taking as much interest in Bob's pumping equipment as he was able, under the circumstances, Jack said, 'the pond will be a real item of beauty in your garden Bob.'

His neighbour paused, then agreed and laughed. 'I thought at first that you said 'a useful facility!'

'That, too,' said Jack very quietly.

19 ~ A Telephone Conversation (His End)

'Hello?'
    'Oh, Victoria.'

'Where am I? Working, of course.

'No, I know I'm not in the office. And if you phoned me there, I do wish you wouldn't -you know I don't like you phoning me at the office.

'Well, I might be in a meeting or seeing someone important and I don't want you phoning me to tell me that your mother is coming to supper or that the cat's been sick or something.'

'Has the cat been sick?

'Oh well, that's all right then.

'Where am I now? I'm working at the flat – thought I'd get a bit of peace and quiet. Its pandemonium in the office today. Miranda's there to take any messages.

'Oh, wasn't she? She must just have popped out to get herself a sandwich or something.

'Down on the first floor to the sandwich bar.

'Tried her three or four times? Oh well – she must have been in one of the other offices.

'I know she's supposed to be in my office all the time – but the secretaries are a bit thin on the ground this week.

'Why? I don't know why. Perhaps there's something going round.

'Well, some bug or other.

'Yes, I'm OK. I know you don't want to catch anything before the Amateur Dramatics put on H.M.S. Pinafore.

'That's a good idea – have a few prophylactic inhalations. Put a towel right over your head.'

'Victoria – I really must go – I've got a lot of work to do here.'

'A woman's voice? Of course you can't – well perhaps you can – it's the television.'

'Yes, I can work with the television on.'

'Well, no, not at home – but I can here.'

'Sounds like someone singing in the shower? Well, it's a seaside programme.'

'I don't know what its called or where it is. Does it matter?'

'Tonight? Well I don't know really – I was thinking that I may even stay here tonight – it will give me a good chance to get this presentation finished. I was going to ring you.'

'Why are you ringing me by the way?'

'Oh, you're not at home? Where are you then?'

'Where? You're coming here?! You're just walking along from the bus stop?!'

'No, no, – that's just fine dear – don't come straight up – I'll meet you downstairs and take you straight out to tea at The Flowered Apron.'

The telephone clicks off. 'Miranda! Quick ! For God's sake get your clothes on and get out of here! Go down the back stairs. Victoria's coming any minute!'

Telephone Conversation (Her End)

'Gerald? I thought I'd get you on your mobile.'
        'Where are you?'

'Yes, I know you're working – but where? You're not in the office.'

'I know you don't like me phoning you at the office – but why not?'

'You can't always be in meetings or seeing important people – I can't think what you do do half the time – and I don't phone you about irrelevant things like my mother coming or the cat being sick. Come to think of it the cat didn't seem quite herself this morning.

'No she hasn't – unless it was out in the garden where I couldn't see her.'

'So where are you now?'

'In the flat to get some peace and quiet? That's a bit odd. And if, as you say, Miranda's in the office to take messages – well, she wasn't there when I phoned.'

'To get a sandwich? Where to?'

'Only down to the first floor? Well, I tried her three or four times – she must eat a lot of sandwiches.'

'In one of the other offices? I thought she was in your office all the time.'

'Why are the secretaries thin on the ground this week?'

'What sort of bug going around?'

'Well, I hope you don't catch it and give it to me – you know that the Amateur Dramatics are doing H.M.S. Pinafore next week – I don't want anything to ruin my performance! Perhaps I had better start taking some inhalations.'

'Yes, I'm sure you have lots of work to do. Gerald, – can I hear a woman's voice?'

'Oh, the television – I thought you couldn't work with the television on – you always say that you find it so distracting.'

'Why is it distracting for you at home but not when you are in the flat? Is someone singing in the shower on the television?'

'A seaside programme oh, – what's it called? Where is it about?'

'No, it doesn't really matter. What time were you planning to get home tonight?'

'Oh, you're staying at the flat? I've left you some ham and salad in the frig at home.'

'Why am I ringing? Oh, yes, – Angela wants me to go shopping with her in town tomorrow – she has to buy an outfit for this wedding she is going to. It will take her ages to choose something. I suggested we meet up early, so I thought that I would stay at the flat tonight and then we can attack the shops as soon as they open in the morning.'

'Where am I now? No, of course I'm not at home – I caught the 3 o'clock train and I'm just walking along from the bus stop to the flat. I have been trying to phone you and tell you my plans many times, but I couldn't get you at the office and your mobile has been switched off.'

'Take me out to tea – that <u>would</u> be nice! All right, I'll meet you in the entrance hall in a few minutes. Bye for the moment.'

Mobile off.

'Miranda in the office all the afternoon my foot!'

Mobile on again.

'Hello? Alistair? Its Victoria. I'm afraid that our arrangement at the flat is off – Gerald is there, and was clearly planning to have a nice cosy time with his little bimbo of a secretary. Now it will just be Gerald and I having an exciting pizza or something.'

Never mind – better luck next time!'

20 ~ The Compensation

Feeling awkward and not a little stupid on his elbow crutches, Guy clicked and clacked himself and his plastered leg along the path by the swimming pool. Not for the first time he cursed under his breath. What bloody awful luck! Just a few days into the holiday and he had to break his leg! Admittedly, if he had been a little more sober when he came out of the taverna, and not showing off quite so stupidly to the girl with blonde hair and navy blue fingernails, he may have coped better with the pile of paving slabs which he encountered on the pavement. These facts, however, did nothing to assuage his self-pity, anger and frustration.

He had received satisfactory treatment at the hospital and the swarthy, curly-headed young doctor had told him, in very passable English, that it was a simple break and would heal in a few weeks. A few weeks! He would have to lug himself about in this plaster for a few weeks! He, who revelled in his fitness and had no time for physical imperfections of any kind, and he – whose holiday was wrecked. He had come to this Greek island with three friends and they were all set to have a very good time. Fat chance about that for him now! And what about hitting it off with the girls? Self confident Guy, with his good looks and quick wit was, in normal circumstances, particularly good at that. One plastered leg would be hampering, to say the very least.

He sighed heavily and leant on his crutches, looking around for somewhere to settle and read his book. How very exciting that will be, he thought bitterly, allowing another great breaker of self-pity to wash over him.

Then he saw the girl. She was lying on a sun bed at the shaded end of the pool. She was alone. She was lovely. He couldn't believe his luck. He propelled himself towards her. 'Hello, beautiful!' he greeted her, 'May I join you?'

'Of course,' she answered, smiling, 'can you manage, with those crutches?'

'It's certainly worth a try!' He carefully manoeuvred himself onto the sun bed next to her. He looked at her in frank admiration, which he felt she could hardly fail to notice. She was beautifully made. Her deep chestnut hair shone and she looked fabulous in a swimsuit of peacock blue.

'Having a good holiday?' he found himself asking, rather conventionally.

'Oh, lovely! How about you?

He found this a disappointingly silly question. How could he be having a good holiday with his leg in plaster for heaven's sake? He launched forth about his misfortune, and she listened patiently. 'So Greece isn't doing me much good, really,' he concluded, 'I can't swim, can't dance, can't go walking, can't fit into the car we've hired and can't even sunbathe without my leg feeling as if it's in a slow oven – anyway – I'd get rather a one-legged tan! I can't even drink very much – in case I fall over and break the other leg! It's all a complete dead loss – I even considered flying home, but that turned out to be rather a complicated and expensive procedure – so I'm sticking the fortnight out –'

' – and trying to make the best of it?' she finished the sentence for him. 'Poor you!' He suddenly realised what a whining bore he was being. Whatever was he thinking about, moaning on about himself to this beautiful girl – it was nothing like his usual approach. 'I'm sorry, I'm not doing a very good job at making the best of it am I?' He tried to excuse himself. 'I'm afraid I haven't got much time for infirmities and disabilities of any description – especially any of my own!'

'But surely you must be able to enjoy something on the island ? The smells and sounds of Greece are so wonderful – the thyme on the hills, steak cooking in herbs, bazuki music, the sea crashing – lots of things – and the warmth of the sun is so lovely – I suppose that's what most of us come for, the sun?'

As she turned towards him two images of his face reflected back at him from her mirrored sunglasses. What colour were her eyes behind them, he wondered – green, brown or even blue? He felt soothed by this girl, and ashamed of his self-centredness. He wanted to do nothing else in the world but stay here, talking with her. 'Forgive me for being such a misery – tell me about you – I don't suppose you are here on holiday by yourself?'

'No, I am here with my sister and brother-in-law. They have just gone to do a bit of shopping and I opted to stay here.'

Lucky for me, thought Guy. 'My three mates have driven off to the hills and then they'll walk for most of the day – I didn't want to cramp their style!' He was even beginning to think that he was enjoying a bit of a bonus. He was looking forward to them coming back, to be able to tell them that he had been chatting up just about the most attractive girl on the complex! 'I'm Guy, by the way, Guy Nicholson.'

'I'm Leah. Good to meet you, Guy.' Nice name, Leah, thought Guy – soft, feminine, suits her.

They chatted away, relaxed and comfortable, their laughter mingling with the sounds of splashes and shouts from the pool. He enjoyed looking at her, and he hoped that she liked what she saw, looking at him. He was quite aware of his physical attributes, as good looking men are, and he felt that this always got him off to quite a good start as far as meeting girls was concerned. But this girl was different. He didn't feel in addition, the need to show off, be tediously witty or to try and impress in a macho kind of way. She was so serene, so composed, and so easy, so very easy to talk to. Even the plaster on his leg felt lighter, and he found that every now and then he almost ceased to be aware of it. He rested his head back on his hands. He had a great desire to know so much more about Leah. He thought of a question . Her answer, maybe, would tell him something interesting about her. 'When you are away,' he asked, turning to her, 'what do you miss most about home?'

Without hesitation the answer came. 'I miss Jess, my guide dog,' she said calmly, with a tender smile.

'Your guide dog?!'

'Yes, you see, I am almost totally blind – sorry, perhaps I ought to have mentioned it before? I can distinguish between light and dark – in fact this bright light makes my eyes feel quite uncomfortable, so I wear these sunglasses. Jess', she continued, 'is my constant companion – it seems strange that she is not under this sun bed now, waiting for me to get up. A white stick is a poor substitute for her. Of course she comes to work with me every day. I work for our local radio station.'

She's blind! Guy amazed to himself – and here she is, appreciating everything when she can't even see *anything* – and here I am, making a fuss about one broken leg! He suddenly felt very humble – and she more amazing. She must have taken his initial silence as a sign of shocked surprise, or even irritation.

' I'm sorry,' she said again, 'I …'

'*You're* sorry!' he said quietly, 'it is I who ought to apologize – for being so crass, for going on so about a perfectly mendable leg. How did you know about it before we even spoke, by the way?'

She laughed. 'I heard you clip clopping along, right from the other end of the pool. When you lose one faculty the remaining ones go into overdrive! Anyway, it was not long before I had a very full explanation! But I also know what aftershave you use, roughly how tall you are, that you probably have quite a good singing voice and an irritating habit of rustling things about in your pocket.'

He grinned like a schoolboy and touched her hand. 'Have you always been blind?' he felt he could ask.

'No, not until I was ten, and then I got meningitis. So I know what everything looks like – faces, colours, the sea, trees, sunsets – everything – I'm very lucky.'

'I think you're amazing,' he said, with feeling.

'Not at all,' she smiled at him, ' but you said that you find it difficult to accept physical imperfections.'

He winced as he recalled his previous, and he realized now, very tactless remark . He would have given anything not to have said it and was aghast at the thought that he had hurt or offended her. How could he make amends? 'All I can say to that

142

is that sometimes something happens that completely changes one's mind about things – especially if they were completely wrong in the first place. Please forgive me.' It was the best he could do. He looked at her. She was smiling. He was conscious of how intensely he wanted things to be all right between them. This was crazy – he had only met her about half an hour ago – and she couldn't even see him!

'It's OK!' She wrinkled a very pretty nose. 'You're quite forgiven! You are probably something like an engineer and you like things to work properly!'

He sighed happily and admitted to working in electronics. They continued to talk and laugh together in the dappled sunshine. Guy began to feel oblivious to his surroundings, apart from Leah, a vision of chestnut hair and peacock swim suit.

Then – 'Leah! We're back!' The sister and her husband were approaching. There were introductions and a brief friendly chat. Then Leah produced a folding white stick from her beach bag. 'Bye, Guy,' she said, 'it has been so nice talking to you.' She slipped her arm through that of her sister's and off they went, chatting happily. Guy watched them go – with an inexplicable sense of loss. He hadn't even asked if he could see her again.

* * * * *

'How's your day been, poor old chap?' his friends asked on their return, exhilarated and sun-tanned.

'I've met the most amazing girl,' was the dreamy answer.

'Well done you – where is she now, then?'

'I don't know – but I shall see her again – hopefully tomorrow. She's beautiful and blind and quite wonderful!'

'Did you say blind?'

'Yes.'

'You – and a blind girl?'

'Mmm – me – I hope me!' Guy grinned at his friends. 'You wait till you meet her!'

He didn't see Leah the next day. Or the next. He sat in the shade by the pool for hours, looking at the first chapter of his book, wearying of the splashes and squeals around him and waiting for her to appear. But no Leah. Tomorrow, he decided, he would seek her out – but he didn't even know her surname! He couldn't, he mused, go crutching around asking if anyone had seen a blind girl! But he would have to do something – he was desperate to see her again. He could not get the thought of her out of his head – her face, her body, her voice, her laugh and just everything about her. However, he did not have to wait much longer – because the next day there she was. And the next. And the next. He proudly introduced her to his mates and watched, smiling as they fell for her charm and he was soon on very friendly terms with her sister and brother-in-law.

By the end of the holiday Guy knew. From way up on his cloud nineteen, he still *really* knew. This wasn't like being with some conquest he had made because she was pretty and amusing and who thought that he was attractive and a bit of a catch. With Leah it was completely different. He basked in her serenity. She had a wholeness about her which he admired and respected and felt that he himself could never attain. She had a sparkle that he could never hope to match. She had a sensitivity and an awareness of life that he would not have thought possible. He needed her more than he ever imagined he could need anything. But in her completeness did she feel that there was any room for him? What a turn up! He would never have imagined that on this holiday he would break a leg and fall in love with a blind girl!

It was their last evening. The soft warm air was full of the smell of thyme. Guy had never really noticed the smell of thyme before – in fact he was finding that there were all sorts of things that he hadn't noticed before. Before Leah.

'I love you, Leah,' he said, uncompromisingly. Have I got any sort of chance?' He looked into the green pools of her eyes. Sightless – and yet somehow they were shining his answer. He raised a hand up to the stars. 'Hey! You up there!' he almost shouted, 'Thanks for a broken leg!'

21 ~ Just as We Are

The worthy members of the Parochial Church Council of St. Bidolph's Church in the parish of Puddle Drayton, left the meeting talking excitedly. It was a snap-cold frosty night and as he locked the presbytery door the vicar watched the retreating figures hurrying through the churchyard, with their breath swirling steam around them.

At the meeting he had read out a letter from the bishop. This concerned a television programme which the BBC plan to make about village churches, to illustrate their present situation, their types of services and their place and influence on rural life. The bishop felt it would be appropriate for St.Bidolph's to take part in the programme – if the PCC and congregation approve.

The vicar, a kindly, gentle man sometimes found his flock a little difficult to manage. Slumped gratefully in a chair by his fireside he said to his wife, 'The PCC certainly seem very enthusiastic about this BBC programme, Alice. I hope its not going to cause a lot of fuss and bother. I'll call a general meeting when we know more details.'

Involuntarily Alice smiled a little knowingly. 'Don't worry about it yet dear, – it might all be lovely. Have a cup of cocoa – it'll warm you up.'

The filming was to take place in the summer, and one early spring evening the vicar, the PCC, and almost the entire congregation of St. Bidolph's were gathered in the church hall to talk about THE PROGRAMME. The mood was expectant. There was a loud hubbub of voices which the vicar eventually managed to subdue by ringing the brass bell on the table in front of him. When he had everyone's attention and before the chatting could start up again, he said, 'As you know, we are here to talk about the proposed television programme in which our church will have a role.'

'A great opportunity for St. Bidolph's!' boomed Captain Roland Morton-Brown, one of the churchwardens sitting beside the vicar.

'So exciting that they have chosen us!' almost squealed Ursula Johnson, the second churchwarden, on the vicar's other side. 'Shall we be able to re-decorate the church before it all happens?'

The vicar held up a hand. 'All we have to do is to enable the people making the programme to film us going about our church work and having our services etc. in our usual way. Just as we are.'

His parishioners dutifully muttered in agreement and then proceeded to bombard him with questions and suggestions.

'When exactly are they coming? We may have to change our holiday!' someone asked.

'Second half of June,' the vicar replied, 'they can't give us an exact date at the moment. Other churches will be taking part also.'

'Will they film the morning service?'

'I think so, yes.'

'Shall we advertise it in the local paper? We want the church to be nice and full.'

'Well, it would be nice if a few more people came than usual – the morning service has been very poorly attended lately, but we certainly won't advertise it.'

'We shall invite our folks down from Sunderland,' announced Mrs Perkins, the church visitor.

'That seems rather a long way to come,' remarked the person sitting next to her.

'I think that we should invite *all* the school children,' enthused Mildred Harrison, the school cleaner, 'the children would love to be on the tele!'

'We could have a bouncy castle in the churchyard!' was the next suggestion.

'No!' the vicar almost shouted, 'It is not a fete. Hardly any of the school children normally come to church. We need to present ourselves *just as we are*.' But his plea was falling on deaf ears.

The organ will need re-tuning,' declared Mrs Hargreaves who had been the organist for the past twenty-five years.

'The churchyard needs more tidying up. The new gardener is expensive,' grumbled Duncan Fraser the treasurer, who guarded the church funds as carefully as he guarded his own.

'We could organise a working party.' suggested Captain Morton-Brown.

'And another to clean the church,' said his fellow churchwarden.

'The film crew will want plenty of beer and sandwiches,' said a farmer's wife, who knew all about beer and sandwiches.

Miss Fortescue, who was in charge of the after-service coffee and biscuits, stood up.

'Talking about refreshments – I shall need some help.'

'Perhaps we ought to get caterers in?' suggested a member who had never enjoyed Miss Fortescue's coffee.

This suggestion was rejected as being expensive and unnecessary. Help would be requested from Mrs Johnson who made very good shortbread and Mrs Rowe who made excellent flapjacks. Everything must be homemade – it was more 'countrified'. The usual custard creams and rich tea biscuits certainly wouldn't do.

'My helpers and I shall fill the church with flowers,' said Marian Postlethwaite, the flower arranger-in-chief, 'it will be a lovely time for garden flowers.'

'*Garden flowers*!' said someone disdainfully. 'Surely we should have proper flowers from the florist?'

'What do you mean – *proper flowers*? What could be more proper than garden flowers in a country church?' Mrs Postlethwaite was outraged.

'Now, now!' the vicar intervened, feeling that he was fast losing control of the meeting, 'garden flowers would be very suitable.' This mollified Mrs Postlethwaite and the treasurer said that in any case florist flowers would be too expensive.

The vicar hurried on to the subject of the music. 'We must have very familiar hymns,' he said. What does our choirmaster suggest?'

Mr Joyce the choirmaster had a lot to suggest. The choir of six persons, including two small boys, was much too minimal. He would invite choirs from other churches to join them. He suggested hymns, psalms, solos, an organ recital and exciting music from the local comprehensive school's brass band which, he assured everyone, was excellent He was sure that Mrs Hargreaves would quite understand if he asked a friend of his, a very gifted organist, to play for the occasion. Mrs Hargreaves did not understand and left the meeting in tears.

'We are not giving a concert, Mr Joyce,' said the vicar despairingly, as his wife hurried after Mrs Hargreaves, 'but having a usual morning service. We shall discuss the music at a later date.'

It was decided to organise a working party to tidy the churchyard and another to spring-clean the church. Someone suggested getting Proclean in, but this expense was vetoed by the treasurer.

After more discussion, argument and, it must be said, some ill-feeling amongst certain persons, the vicar brought the meeting to a close with a hasty prayer, which mentioned tolerance, love and humility.

* * * * *

Some weeks later the vicar and his wife settled in front of the television to watch the resultant programme. There were all too fleeting glimpses of their church, crammed with people, many of whom they did not even recognise. There were scouts, guides, brownies, cubs, beavers and rainbows. Some members of the congregation had arrived exceedingly early, to secure a place in front of a camera. There they sat, in their best outfits, looking particularly devout. They sang the hymns with widely opened mouths and exaggerated articulation.

'They look like a row of fish!' laughed Alice.

Flowers cascaded from every nook and cranny – unfortunate for the hay fever sufferers.

The visiting gifted organist played enthusiastically but much too loudly. The chancel was crowded with a massed choir and the school brass band, conducted by an almost manic Mr Joyce. There was a shot of the vicar in pristine vestments commencing his sermon. He thought his voice sounded very strange and high-pitched His congregation appeared to be hanging on his every word.

Alas! There was no coverage of the special refreshments and only for seconds had the camera passed over the beautifully mown churchyard. However, it had lingered on some brasses which were gleaming as they had seldom gleamed before.

As the programme ended with the sound of peeling bells from another church, the vicar reached for the off switch. 'Well', he sighed, 'I have dreamt of achieving those sort of services for ten years – and it took just one television programme! But that was certainly not us as we *really* are – everyone dancing to their own holy tune for the benefit of the tele. It was a hypocritical farce! I'm afraid I lost all control of it.'

Alice smiled a tolerant smile, 'Perhaps, dear, that *is* how we really are – just wanting a little bit of personal glory – its surely human nature?'

'What! Pretending? Putting on a show – supposedly to the Glory of the Lord?'

'Yes.'

'And quarrelling to boot?

'That as well. We have feet of clay.'

'You will have to help me calm the ill-feeling *and* the self-exultation!'

'Of course. But just think – we have, hopefully, a satisfied bishop, a sparkling clean church, an immaculate churchyard – and I think that you looked *great* on the tele – let's count our blessings!'

22 ~ From A Victorian Lady's Diary

The Laurels

Fordwyche Road.

Sydenham.

Thursday 12th. October 1886.

Woke to Cedric's snoring and the first frost of the season. Hadn't asked the gardener to bring geraniums in. Bedroom very chill – must start having fires lit upstairs – all that mess of coal and ashes up and down the back stairs and Annie grumbling. Annie doesn't grumble much out loud but very effectively in silence.

Children very noisy – new Nanny hopeless, not firm enough and takes no notice of what I say. Never quite sure why the last Nanny left. She hadn't been here very long.

Changes cannot be good for the children. I wish Cedric would get involved a little more, then *he* could speak to Nanny – but says it is not his ' area'. I know he works very hard in his City office. I don't really know much about his work. If I ask him he says I wouldn't understand – so I suppose I wouldn't. My job is to run the house and cope with the children – but I find it very burdensome and often more than I can manage, even though I have a house of only moderate size, three living-in servants, a gardener and a cleaning woman. Mrs Digby-Smythe has a far larger house than mine, more servants to worry about *and* more children – yet seems to be so calm and 'in control' all the time.

I wish I was like Mrs Digby-Smythe.

My dinner party is tomorrow! Have changed my mind about the menu so many times and cannot remember quite what was decided upon. Cook being unpleasant and difficult. Oh dear!

What if the Morrisons don't get on with the Rees-Martins? Or Councillor Albert Rigby, after a glass or two of wine, becomes too verbose and boring about the present local government situation? I hope Dr Harrington doesn't fall asleep, which has been known. The poor man works too hard. His wife cannot come as she has gone to stay with her sister who is ill, so Dr Harrington is coming with the young man who has arrived to be his assistant. Have invited the new young schoolmistress, hoping they will be agreeable together.

Downstairs to see Cook after breakfast. How can she be domineering, disapproving and servile at one and the same time? Went through dinner party menu (again). Menu settled. Asparagus soup, (found a new recipe, but Cook said she would only do the one she was used to) smoked trout, (no comment from Cook) duck with orange sauce, (a great deal of comment from Cook) lemon soufflé and a cheese board. Cook still not happy about the soufflé. Would prefer to do trifle. Stood my ground. Trifle rather 'ordinary.' Said I would come and do the soufflés myself (not that I'm quite sure how to) but Cook said she would manage somehow, thank you. Quite shaky as I emerged gratefully from the kitchen. Met by Annie saying that the Vicar had called and was in the drawing room. Greeted Vicar, conscious that the drawing room still untidy from activities of the day before and with dust gleaming defiantly in wintry sunshine.

Why do people call so *early*? The Vicar wants me to help with distribution of charity parcels next week. Mrs Digby-Smythe is organising it. Say I will. The Vicar thinks I have more time to spare for charity work than I feel is reasonable. Must complain to Annie about state of drawing room.

Nanny very cross. Children didn't want morning walk. Bertram particularly difficult. Baby is teething and Arabella having so many tantrums lately. Needed to go to drapers to get ribbon for blue dress to wear tomorrow, so take children with me.

Letter from Mama arrived by second post. Aunt Gertrude is staying with her and they are coming to tea this afternoon as they want to see the children! I prayed that they would behave. Mama can be quite critical of them. And of me.

Persuade Cook to make a cake and I put together some cucumber sandwiches as daintily as possible (not very). Gave Cook mollifying afternoon off.

Tea episode fairly tolerable. Children mercifully over-awed by formidable Aunt Gertrude and their behaviour, apart from making frightful faces when they thought no one was looking, was acceptably subdued. Baby slept most of the time, partly due to exhaustion and also to the effect of a few drops of brandy in his lunchtime bottle.

Mama seemed quite approving of the children, even if not of the cucumber sandwiches, which admittedly, tended to fall apart.

Blue ribbon does not match blue dress. Will have to wear green dress.

Saturday October 14th.

Too exhausted last night to write diary.

After breakfast yesterday Nanny gave notice. Children too naughty, household too disorganised, plus several other reasons I cannot remember. She'll work a week's notice. Agency again – oh dear.

Dinner party day. Urged Annie and Mrs Roberts to clean drawing-room, dining-room and then the silver. They made me feel like an Egyptian slave-driver. Mrs Roberts says her bunions are worse.

Kitchen intimidating hive of activity. Agency sent a kitchen maid to help Cook, who declared that *twelve* persons was too many for *one* person to cook for. Don't think that kitchen maid is likely to come again.

Delivery arrived – insufficient asparagus, too many trout, oranges, no lemons. Cook fussed about the dirt the gardener brought in with the vegetables; needed more herbs; when were the ducks coming? Etc.

Wanted to flee from the kitchen like Lot's wife from Sodom. If I were turned into a pillar of salt at least I would have to give no more dinner parties.

Mrs Digby-Smythe called in the morning, whilst discordant sounds came from music room via Arabella, Nanny was screaming at Bertram who was being particularly wilful and Mrs Roberts shuffled along the hall, slopping out the contents of a pail of dirty water as she went. Showed Mrs Digby-Smythe into the drawing-room, encountering Annie sprawled in an armchair looking at a dubious-natured magazine. Annie scuttled off, Mrs Digby-Smythe smiled sweetly, remarking, sympathetically, how difficult servants can be these days and explained about the distribution of the charity parcels. As she took her leave she thanked me graciously for being willing to help. Felt guilty about my initial grudging attitude.

Panicked through the rest of the day – punctuated by crises in the kitchen, chaos in the nursery, constant nagging at poor Annie and Mrs Roberts and being jolted into remembering all the things I had forgotten. Had failed to order hot-house flowers, so made do with obliging leaves and red berries from garden. Laid table myself – *very* carefully, as at my last dinner party there were omissions, causing some confusion and Cedric displeased. Conviction that I am not the material that a successful hostess, mother, wife or housekeeper is made of re-enforced.

Cedric home on early train. Children persuaded into bed. Failed to calm Cook.

Put on green dress (not as nice as blue). New stays too tight.

Dinner party not a disaster! Cook, despite everything had done very well. The asparagus soup was a very good flavour but could have been a bit hotter but the trout and the duck were excellent. The soufflé had sunk a little but I don't think that anyone noticed.

Cedric presided happily at the head of the table, and I at the foot, grateful that only minimal contributions to conversation were required of me. Dr Harrington sat sleepily on my right, content not to be taxed with small-talk and Councillor Rigby on my left waxed eloquent on subjects such as water supply, the building of the workhouse, idleness of the poor, performance of the church choir and plans for the new Town Hall. And other things. Thankfully I had to say little as he does not take kindly to interruption. Our guests listened to him with apparent interest. Dr Harrington's assistant (Henry Standing) and the new schoolmistress (Mary Woods) appeared to get on very well together, which was pleasing. Hopefully, only I was conscious of the muffled clatter from the kitchen, intermittent cries from the nursery and the strands of hair escaping from underneath Annie's cap.

The gentlemen mellowed over port, and we ladies had coffee in the drawing-room, which went satisfactorily, apart from Mrs Rigby complaining about the poor standard of behaviour of the children at the school – which was a bit unfair to Mary Woods has she has only recently arrived and is an extremely pleasant person altogether. Neither Annie or I spilt the coffee and I was grateful how blemishes in rooms dim in the light of oil lamps. I think our guests all enjoyed the evening and it was quite late when everyone left. If guests leave early one feels that they cannot wait to get home because they have not found things very pleasant. Dr Harrington did leave a little earlier – but he was very tired and had surgery in the morning. Henry Stanton, I noted, was pleased to escort Mary Woods back to School Cottage.

Moonlight lit the drive and the frosted geraniums as we went back into the house. Cedric took my hand. 'Well done, my dear,' he said. Praise enough!

This morning I thanked Cook warmly for yesterday, and she was pleased. Must create a happier working relationship with Cook. I think her bark is worse than her bite.

Am not sorry Nanny is leaving. Will spend more time with the children myself – am sure that will be better. Will help distribute the charity parcels with a good heart and be thankful for my own blessings. Must try not to feel a failure all the time. Anyway, I am not a failure *all* the time.

But I still wish I was more like Mrs Digby-Smythe.

23 ~ Going To Auntie Margaret's

'There you are – all strapped in. Have you got Scruffy and Tumble?'

'Yes.'

'Good. Off we go then.'

'Mummy, where are we going?'

'We're going to Auntie Margaret's.'

'Why?'

'Because she wants to see us.'

'But she knows what we look like. Why does she want to look at us again?'

'She doesn't just want to look at us – she wants to talk to us as well.'

'Why?'

'Because she does.'

But she doesn't talk to me much – she only talks to you. And I haven't got anything to play with.'

'Yes you have – you've got Scruffy dog and Tumble the clown and I have brought some of your picture books in this bag.'

'Can we go to the park?'

'Perhaps we can – after lunch.'

'What are we going to have for lunch?"

'I don't know.'

'Perhaps we'll have sausages?'

'No, we won't have sausages.'

'Why?'

'Because Margaret is a vegetarian.'

'I thought she was an auntie. What's a veg-et-er-train?'

'A veg-et-arian. Its someone who doesn't eat any meat and eats lots of fruit and vegetables instead.'

'Even instead of sausages?'

'Yes.'

'So what do they eat?'

'What I said – fruit and vegetables – carrots and cabbage and peas and apples and oranges and things like that.'

'And bananas?'

'Yes.'

'And pears?'

'Yes.'

'And beans?'

'Yes.'

'And horrible spinach?'

'Spinach isn't horrible.'

'I think its horrible.'

'Spinach is very good for you.'

'But that doesn't stop it from being horrible. Anyway, I want sausages for lunch.'

'We won't be having sausages – and you're not to make a fuss about lunch and just eat what Auntie Margaret gives you, then if we go to the park you can have an ice cream.'

'Why doesn't Auntie Margaret like sausages?'

'Because she thinks that it is better to eat fruit and vegetables.'

'Oh, Mummy, why are you stopping?'

'Because we are at a crossing, where people can walk over to the other side of the road. When the lights are red all the cars and lorries have got to stop to let the people walk over the road and then when the lights are green the cars can go again – like we have got at home and we can go when the little green man lights up.'

'The lights have turned green now – why aren't you going?'

'Because I am waiting for that elderly lady to finish crossing the road.'

'Is she walking slowly because she is an old lady?'

'Yes.

A pause.

'Mummy?'

'Yes?'

'You're quite a new lady aren't you?'

'I'd like to think so.'

'Why do some people get old?'

'Everyone gets old – slowly. We all start off as babies and the girl babies grow up into little girls and go to school and the boy babies grow up into little boys and go to school, and then the girls grow up into mummies and the boys grow up into daddies.'

'Oh – and then the mummies have more girl babies and the daddies have more boy babies?'

'No. Only mummies have babies.'

'Why?'

'Because babies grow in the mummies' tummies and the daddies haven't got the right sort of tummies.'

'Why?

'Because that is how God has made them.'

'Oh. Look Mummy – why is that dog pulling that lady along?'

'I think that the lady might be taking the dog for a walk in the park and the dog is in a hurry to get there.'

'Can we stop and go to the park?

'No. We are going to Auntie Margaret's first.'

'Oh – *please*'

'I said No and I mean No.'

'Can I have a drink?'

'There's some orange in the bottle there on the seat.'

'It's fallen on the floor.'

'Well I can't stop now– we'll have to wait until there's a lay-by.'

'What's a lay-by?'

'It's a space by the side of the road where you can stop the car, get out and pick up bottles of orange drink that have fallen on the floor.'

'Is that all you can do in a lay-by?'

'No, but it's all that we're going to do.

'Mummy – what are all those white stones sticking up out of the grass?'

'Where?'

'Over there.'

'That's a graveyard.'

'What's a graveyard?'

'It's a place where people are buried when they have died. Do you remember when Hammy the Hamster died and we put him in a cardboard box and we put that in a hole that Daddy dug in the garden?'

'Yes, and I was sad.'

'And so that's what happens when people die. They are put in a very special posh wooden box and are buried in a graveyard usually next to a church.'

'But what are the white stones for?'

'They have got the people's names on them.

'But if the people are dead they don't have to know what their names are any more.'

'No, but their friends and relations need to know.'

'But they know already.'

'Yes but the friends and relations want to come and think about them and leave some flowers and so they want to know where to leave the flowers.'

'Oh.'

'Here's a lay-by. I'll stop and you can have a drink. And do you want to do a wee?'

'No.'

'Are you sure?'

'Yes.'

'Right – here's your drink, and it shouldn't be too long before we get to Auntie Margaret's. OK?'

'Yes.'

'Off we go then.'

'Mummy?'

'Yes?'

'I don't believe in Father Christmas.'

'Don't you? Why not?'

'Because if he goes down everybody's chimney he would get very sooty and you never see a Father Christmas sooty. And anyway my friend Emily at Nursery School hasn't got a chimney in her house and she and her brother Tom still got presents. So I think its *pretend*.'

'I see. But its ages and ages until Christmas – so you needn't think much about it now.'

'Oh Mummy look – there's a *really* big van. What's it for?'

'It's a removal van – someone's moving house.'

'How can you move a house?'

'You don't move the house – just the furniture and things inside it. They are taken to another house where the people are going to live and all put into that.'

'Are we going to move house?'

'No.'

'Good. I don't want to move house.'

'That's just as well then – and here we are at Auntie Margaret's house.'

'I hope that she has forgotten that she doesn't eat sausages'

'Don't forget what I said about lunch.'

'Only if we can go to the park afterwards and I can have an ice cream.

'Well, – you've been very good on the journey – so we'll see, shall we?'

24 ~ The Duchess

Mary knew that Tom almost lived and breathed engines as soon as she met him at a friend's party all those years ago. Their initial conversation had centred around the second-hand motor bike of which he was the proud new owner. Subsequently, when he took her out there was no point in wearing a pretty dress or having her hair done, as she always had to don trousers, an overlarge jacket and a crash helmet Tom worked in heavy engineering and his recreation mostly consisted of 'fixing engines' or mutilating them and rearranging some of their component parts into others. Tom's hands were permanently impregnated with a grime which seemed never to be completely dislodged even after quite rigorous treatment with a scrubbing brush and detergents of various kinds. Tom's person had about it a faint aroma of engine oil which he did not even attempt to camouflage with anything which he derisively described as 'scent'.

But Tom, ruggedly handsome, was kind and tolerant, generous and warm-hearted and fun to be with. He loved Mary and asked her to marry him. So she did, with his obsession with engines as part of the package.

When they had settled in their first home Mary thought that other things would occupy Tom's spare time – like decorating, putting up shelves and tiling the bathroom.

But these sort of domestic chores had very little appeal for Tom, although he would eventually get around to doing them (not particularly well) after she had pestered him enough. He was much happier in the garage, most of which he had commandeered as a workshop. There was never room for even the front bumper of the car.

Pregnant with their first baby Mary thought that becoming a father would dilute Tom's mechanical obsession and may really change things. It did, of course, babies always do, and Tom was thrilled with Joss, his baby son from the moment he first held him in his big strong grimy hands, imbuing the new white blanket with the smell of engine oil. So now he had a baby to love *as well* as his wife and his engines and he felt himself fortunate indeed!

Shortly after their second son Jake was born they were able to afford a larger house. They found one which suited them well, on the outskirts of the town, bordering on fields and with a good sized garden.

'We can really make this garden lovely!' said Mary, who enjoyed gardening and was glowing with excitement.

'There is plenty of room for me to have a nice big workshop!' said Tom, busy with his own thoughts and not listening to Mary, 'and perhaps I could get hold of a second-hand ride-on mower – that would make an easy job of the grass, as long as we don't have flower beds and things getting in the way.'

Mary realized that she and Tom were going to have very different ideas about the garden and that the only interest and pleasure that Tom was going to experience from it would be when wielding some sort of machinery around it – or when necessary 'fixing' some sort of machinery which he could wield around it. Somehow there would have to be a compromise.

Life with a new house and two small sons was busy, but somehow Tom managed to build his workshop into which he disappeared as often as possible and Mary created borders and beds in the garden which the sit-on mower could sweep around fairly easily.

Joss was now a lively toddler and if Mary asked Tom to look after him, he would take him into the workshop, fasten him into his little chair and give him a toy hammer to bang on its table, or give him a plastic hammer and screws to play with. When Joss wearied of that he would be put in the motorised wheelbarrow and zoomed around the garden which caused him to squeal with delight.

Soon Jake was banging a hammer clutched in a small plump hand, and clammering for rides in the wheelbarrow. Toys were investigated, pulled apart and attempts made to put them together again; pedal cars were raced around the garden; tool boxes were given at present times; filthy dungarees were forever chugging in the washing machine and dirty finger marks were forever appearing on doors and walls. The boys chose to do metalwork at school and Mary received some strangely shaped metallic objects, lovingly wrapped in gift paper and proudly presented to her at birthdays and at Christmastime.

Joss and Jake were certainly their father's sons.

Installed happily in his workshop Tom had taken up model engineering, spending painstaking hours commencing to make a scale model of The Flying Scotsman.

Mary still could not muster up much interest in the engineering activities which so occupied Tom and the boys. Used to it as she was, she often found herself feeling somewhat resentful that they were not doing other things as a family – which included her! She expressed this feeling to her mother one day.

'Better to share Tom with cogs, pistons and a metal turning lathe than with another woman!' was her mother's reply, 'Tom is a dear and a good husband and father. His passion for all things mechanical is all part of the deal – you knew that when you married him. Off you go and count your blessings.'

So she did. She went to interior design and upholstery classes, agreed to be the secretary of the local Save The Children committee and joined the garden and flower arranging clubs. So she had her own interests, whilst Tom, Joss and Jake and now 'The Flying Scotsman' had theirs. She was now a very enthusiastic gardener, creating a rockery, a herb garden and more flower beds. Climbing plants covered fences and walls and from spring to autumn flowers tumbled out of pots and urns and hanging baskets. It was not so easy for Tom to cut the grass, but he didn't grumble too much and appreciated her gardening efforts nonetheless.

One day one of the boys spilt some very dirty and very nasty engine oil over a shrub which Mary had planted two years previously and which was just about to bloom for the first time. Mary could see it practically turning up its toes and dying before her eyes and she was very cross.

'Look what you've done to my viburnum!' she shrilled.

'Your what, Mum?' questioned Joss, looking up innocently enough from some greasy-looking piece of metal he was holding.

'This plant here – its had this disgusting oil poured all over it – it will never survive. All you three think about are bits of metal. I feel that your brains must be fixed together with nuts and bolts. Can't you think of anything else?'

'Now Mary love, its not like you to get upset like this,' said Tom soothingly.

Mary didn't want to be soothed. 'Yes it is – I do get upset – and I'm upset now! And you two boys are as obsessional as your father!'

'Tell you what,' said Tom, feeling that an olive branch of some sort needed to be offered. 'Why don't you come to the traction engine rally with us tomorrow – there is a really big one at Bennington – only about ten miles away. You never come with us and they are really great.'

'But I'm not interested in traction engines.'

'Oh, come on, love – we can take a picnic and we can stop at the garden centre on the way back and get a couple more shrubs in place of you vi-thingy.'

'Jake and I will buy you one each,' enticed Joss, 'anyway you'll probably enjoy the rally when you get there!'

Mary grudgingly accepted the olive branch and said she would go, secretly knowing that she would prefer a day in the garden or an opportunity to finish wallpapering the spare bedroom.

The traction engine rally was blessed with a fine day and crowds of people. Three large fields were a moving mass of colour and noise. There was a smell of coal and oil and steam. A carousel was turning to the music of its mechanical organ. Huge traction engines were hissing and chuffing. There were side stalls of all varieties and the vendors were shouting about their wares. Vintage cars and yesterday's motor bikes, fire engines, commercial vans and tractors were standing in polished rows, gleaming in the sun. Small stationary generators chugged away – some quite gently and others in fits and starts. Whistles and hooters were sounding and the public address system was blasting and crackling and difficult to decipher. Dogs, straining on their leads were frustratedly barking at each other and waving and laughing children were having rides on a model train. The train was being driven by the proud owner, sitting astride his creation which had probably taken him twenty years to build. In his peaked cap and overalls he was probably enjoying himself even more than the children were.

In spite of her declared disinterest Mary could not help becoming caught up in the atmosphere, the enthusiasm and the enjoyment of watching people having a good time.

Tom and the boys were engrossed in looking at a stall piled high with tools and engine components. Mary, bored with the tools and lured by the music, wandered off in the direction of the carousel.

And there she saw it – the most magnificent Burrell's Showmans Engine.

It was resplendent in its red and gold enamelled paintwork and shining brass. She marvelled at its great wheels, its furnace and its mass of cogs, tubes and pistons. Everything about it was immaculate. Well steamed up, the engine was running beautifully, and what was so impressive was that it was almost silent. Mesmerised, Mary watched the well-greased piston rods gliding backwards and forwards making a soft rhythmic chuff as steam met metal and at the slow turn of the fly wheel as the cogs connected with absolute perfection. The big belt whirred as it transferred its power to the generator, providing energy to drive the carousel and play its colourful organ. It was so powerful – and yet so gentle and smooth. Mary read the information placard about it. It had been manufactured early in the 20th. Century in Sheffield, the city built on iron and steel and at a time when England led the world in heavy engineering skill. The maker's name was proudly displayed in beautiful gold lettering more gold lettering stated 'Mighty in Strength and Endurance.'

Mary gazed at the engine for a long time. She felt strangely moved. For the first time she began to understand the tremendous achievement, excitement, skill and fascination involved in engineering – and yes – even romance – she could understand how an enthusiast could have a love affair with a machine such as this! She felt so pleased and oddly grateful that dedicated people had restored it to its former glory. She thought of the time when life was so much less sophisticated and the fair came to town – when at night hundreds of lights lit a green or a park and the Showman's Engine would be in full steam, the music playing, the carousel turning and the swing boats reaching up to the stars. How exciting it must have been!

'Oh there you are Mum – we've been looking for you for about the last half an hour!'

She came out of her reverie and turned to her three boys, her eyes shining inexplicably, with tears. 'Isn't it just beautiful?' she said.

They looked at her in undisguised amazement.

* * * * *

It was some months later and Tom came home late for supper.

'Where've you been, Dad?' asked Jake.

'I've been buying a traction engine,' Tom replied, with a straight face, as if he had just bought a pair of socks.

'Pull the other one, Dad,' from Joss.

'No, straight up!' Tom almost whooped.

The boys stared at him open mouthed and Mary who had just come into the room with an casserole pot almost dropped it.

Tom's eyes shone as he plonked himself down at the table. 'I met a chap in the pub the other day, who knew another chap who said that there was some sort of engine that had been in a disused barn in one of his fields for as long as he could remember. He had taken the farm over from his father years ago. I thought that it might be worth a look.'

I didn't say anything to you lot in case it wouldn't come to anything – and if it did, well then I could spring a surprise! I left work early today and went to see it – and its ours!!'

Tom was then bombarded with questions. 'What sort? What condition? When can we see it? Where is it? How can we get it? Where can we put it? (This from Mary, fearing for her lawn.)

'It's a road locomotive – the sort that used to be taken from farm to farm to generate electricity for threshing machines and suchlike. It's in very poor condition and the farmer didn't want very much for it – he was glad to get rid of it and seemed rather surprised that I wanted it at all. I could just make out through the rust that she is called 'The Duchess.'

'Grand or what?' said Jake.

'Its about time we had another female in this household!' said Mary.

'We'll get her up great!' Joss yelled, punching the air.

'It'll take a long time,' warned Tom, 'but I can start tomorrow by finding out about a tractor and trailer and some very heavy lifting gear to move her. I'll twist Frank Stewart's arm about letting us putting it by our fence in his field. I shouldn't think that it'll take more than a couple of beers – he's a good sort and the field is set aside. I think that he'll probably be quite interested in the engine anyway.'

So The Duchess joined the family – poor, rusty, neglected-for-decades Duchess.

It took four years for her to begin to recover her former glory. Hundreds of hours work and much patience and skill. Some of her components were rusted beyond repair and had to be replaced to the original specification, and it seemed to Mary that most of the rest had to be removed, cleaned and soaked in oil and then put back again.

It was a wonderful engineering experience for the boys and they both had a year out before they went to university to devote to the now beloved engine. They didn't help to save the Third World, but they did help to save The Duchess.

Tom put his model of The Flying Scotsman well on the back burner and threw his heart and soul into 'the real thing.'

Mary worked on The Duchess as enthusiastically as anyone. The weeds thrived in her garden whilst she worked her way through a small mountain of wire wool rubbing down rust; she gave up her classes and spent hours working on The Duchess's brass, and later, instead of re-decorating the sitting room she was helping to paint The Duchess's bodywork in her original colours of green, black and gold. It was a meticulous job and the services of a professional was obtained to do the decorative lines and embellishments in gold.

Joss by this time had acquired a girlfriend called Ruth. Her general suitability as far as the others were concerned was judged by the amount of enthusiasm she had concerning The Duchess – which wasn't, it was deemed, quite enough. Mary had trodden that road and hadn't got it quite right, but she held her counsel – there was time.

At last the day came when The Duchess was to be shown for the first time at a traction engine rally. The family were as excited as if they were having a wedding.

The Duchess was gleaming and steamed up perfectly. She was announced over the P.A. system as if she was arriving at a ball. With a burst of steam and her whistle blowing, into the arena she came. What a triumph for the family!

Tom was stoking her fire, Joss and Jake were riding behind – but it was Mary who was at the wheel of The Duchess. Mary, who did not think that she liked engines and who had suffered them as unspeaking rivals for years. Mary, in her dungarees, her hair stuffed into a peaked cap, her face smeared with tears and coal dust and beaming with happiness and pride. They waved to the cheering enthusiastic crowd as The Duchess circled round the arena. It was a moment that that they would all forever cherish.

'Obsessions,' stated Mary later, when they had clambered down from The Duchess and she was pouring tea out of a thermos flask, 'should always be shared – then they don't seem like obsessions at all!'

Then she kissed the other three shining grimy faces in turn.

25 ~ The Swing

It was high summer when we moved into the house and the long sunny days welcomed us into the country from the town. The house was on the edge of the village and fields and meadows edged away from its overgrown garden. Our three children thought that we had moved into heaven.

The house had been empty for a long time and time never treats empty houses kindly. It was the school holidays. Whilst the children happily explored their new environment Jeff and I practically wore ourselves out cleaning and unpacking and trying to get the house and our possessions in some sort of order.

On our second evening, after the children had eventually sunk into an exhausted sleep in their somewhat makeshift bedrooms, we managed to unearth a bottle of wine. We took our glasses outside and sitting on a couple of upturned boxes, we drank a toast to ourselves and to our move. The evening was warm and soft and still – quite perfect, and we felt very tired but very happy.

'It's a dear house,' I said, 'but I feel that there is something sad about it – I suppose because it's been empty, houses don't like that. I hope it's pleased that we've come to make it happy again.'

'You sentimental old silly,' Jeff replied, as kissed me, 'but it's a good house for us – we're very lucky – although it's going to keep us busy – for ages. Let's heat up one of those pizzas and then I'm for bed.'

During that night I was woken by a sharp eerie cry – it sounded just below our window.

'Whatever was that?' I cried out.

'I think it was a vixen calling,' said Jeff sleepily, 'you'll have to get used to the sounds of the country.'

Jeff went to sleep again immediately, as men seem able to do, but I laid awake, listening to the sounds of the night and thinking about the house and all the things we needed to do the next day. I thought that the vixen called again, farther away now, and then I heard one of the children crying. I padded into their rooms but each was fast asleep, with bare limbs spread-eagled out into the close warmth of the night. I was sure I had heard one of them crying.

The following day we continued unpacking and cleaning, in order to make the house feel a bit more like home. Jeff spent a long time coaxing the old left-behind cooker to work. Behind it we found two little toy cars which I washed and put in the toy box.

The children were playing in the meadow beyond the garden and I wandered down the to call them to come and get a sandwich for lunch.

The garden was going to be quite a challenge. It was difficult to work out exactly where grass, flower beds and paths may have been. There was a lovely old apple tree in one corner promising a good crop of fruit later on. There was a good sturdy branch where we had hung the children's swing, but another large branch must have broken off and its jagged remains were left jutting out of the trunk.

The children were playing in the far end of the meadow. I could hear them shouting and saw their heads bobbing about in the long grasses. Then I saw a fourth head – fair, curly, some distance away from the others. 'That's good,' I thought, 'they are making friends with one of the other children in the village – perhaps I'll need to make some more sandwiches.' I shouted at them to come in, received an answering wave and went back to the house.

'Has the little boy you were playing with gone home?' I asked, when three grubby figures appeared in the kitchen and the usual coercion concerning hand-washing had been applied. I received looks reserved for mothers whose children consider that they are losing a grasp on life. 'Don't be silly, Mum – there was only us in the meadow.'

Strange – I was sure another child was there. I shooed the children out into the garden with their sandwiches and the incident went from my mind.

A few days later I came back from the village shop with as much shopping as I could carry. Everyone seemed so friendly. The nice lady at the check-out asked me which house we had moved into. I had the feeling that she was a little quiet when I told her and that just momentarily her cheerful face clouded a little. But at the time there was some confusion about the price of tomatoes and I thought no more about it.

When I reached the house and had relieved myself of my shopping bags I went out into the garden to see what Jeff and the children were up to. I couldn't see them anywhere.

Then I heard the squeak of the swing on the apple tree – but when I reached it no one was there. The empty swing was gently moving to and fro. To and fro.

26 ~ The Reward

Holding her protesting baby under one arm, Jane dragged the bag-laden buggy over the sand dunes with the other. The children trailed behind carrying bottles of drink, buckets and spades, towels and swim suits.

They reached the top of the dunes – and there was the sea – diamond-sparkling, gently whooshing at the sun-kissed sand and pebbles at its edge. Thankfully Jane relieved her aching arms of their burdens.

The boys – Jane's son Ben and his friend Tom, were soon into their swimming trunks and in a flurry of tossed-up sand ran down the beach. Ben had insisted on Tom coming with them today – he wasn't going on a picnic 'just with girls and a baby.'

'I don't like the smell of the seaweed, Mummy,' complained Anna.

'Seaweed is all part of the seaside, you have to put up with it.' her mother replied. 'Help me spread this rug, and then put some sun cream on.'

Jane rescued the crawling-away baby who was investigating the comestible properties of sand. She strapped him back in his buggy, which made him scream in fury.

'Sally, would you like to come to the sea with me?' Anna asked.

Sally, slowly letting sand run like disappearing silk through her fingers, shook her head.

She had been placed as a foster child with the family a week ago. She had not yet spoken one word.

'If you're going, Anna, just paddle and stay where I can see you. ' Jane said. 'Now Sally, shall we get the picnic ready?'

Silently Sally dived into plastic bags, producing packets of crisps and boxes of sandwiches. Anna soon reappeared. 'The boys kept splashing me,' she complained, 'I hate them.'

'No you don't,' rejoined her mother, picking up a towel, 'dry yourself a bit and sit down next to Sally and have something to eat.'

The baby, frustrated in the confines of his buggy demanded to be released. He was put on the rug and given a biscuit which he immediately dunked in the sand.

The boys came zooming back, laughing and shivering, dripping onto the rug.

'Go away – you're *horrible*!' shouted Anna.

Jane did her best to calm everyone down, smiling at Sally and dispensing towels, food, drink, instructions and good cheer.

'These crisps are salt and vinegar!' complained Ben, as if they were coated in arsenic.

'Yuck!'

'I'll have them then – they're my best,' Said Tom obligingly. During the transfer most of the crisps fell out of the packet and the baby knocked a beaker of orange juice over in an attempt to retrieve some. The next complaint was that the sandwiches had gathered sand. Sally, munching into her sandwich, sandy or not, wriggled her feet in and out of the sand in a world of her own.

The baby kept clawing his sun hat off and was unable to understand why he wasn't allowed to crawl around at his pleasure. The sand was attracted to him like iron filings to a magnet. In fact the sand was attracted to everything like iron filings to a magnet.

Jane decided that babies and beaches were not a very good mix, and wondered why ever she had thought this picnic such a good idea!

No one was very keen to eat the cold burnt sausages, Jane found that she had not brought a knife with which to slice the cucumber and looking at fingers and faces realised that it was a mistake to bring the packet of chocolate biscuits. But it was not until a box of jam tarts was opened that the wasps arrived on the scene. With sinister humming they glided, hovered and dived around, undeterred by frantic waving of hands and flapping of beach towels. Jane then decide that everyone had consumed enough food to sustain them for the time being, and bundled the debris away from the threatening wasps, stuffing everything unceremoniously in accommodating plastic bags.

This was timely, as just then a very large, very wet and very friendly dog came bounding out of the sea, anxious for a game with any human who was willing. Barking excitedly, he gave himself an extremely hearty shake, showering the picnic party with a mixture of salt water, sand and dog hairs.

The boys went off to play with the dog, and all three had a jolly time until the dog punctured the beach ball. Attention was then given to building sand castles, and Anna collected shells in her bucket.

'Sally, come and have a paddle with me,' Jane persuaded. Sally looked up and nodded her head. Jane picked up her poor frustrated baby and took Sally by the hand.

When they reached the water's edge, Jane felt a little thrill of pleasure go through Sally as the gentle waves caressed her feet. She gasped and chuckled as the larger ones splashed up to her knees. She dug her toes into the wet sand and watched as the waves evened out the holes she had made. She bent down to touch the water with her hands and pick up pebbles, to watch them splash when she threw them back into the sea. She popped the seaweed bladders, squealed at the tiny crabs and was fascinated when the wheeling, crying seagulls landed on the water so near to her. They dipped the baby's feet in the water which made him chuckle in amazement, and Sally gave him a wet, sandy hug which he seemed to appreciate in the spirit in which it was given. Then they were joined by Anna with her bucket of shells – except that most of them were little live sea snails which were crawling away, desperately trying to escape from the bucket and return to their habitat. This made the little girls laugh and laugh together.

'The boys are making a good sand castle, Sally – come and see!' Anna said. They both went running up the beach, to be met by the boys who said that the dog had peed over the castle so they had stopped building it. Shortly after this the sun suddenly went in and the beach lost its glow and the sea its sparkle. Jane looked at the sky and saw ominous clouds approaching, meaning that the weather was going to change very rapidly.

'That's all we need!' she muttered under her breath, and then, Come on children – I think its going to rain – we better pack up quickly and get back to the car!'

The scramble to collect possessions together began. People were leaving the beach looking like a scattered swarm of burdened ants. Jane and her entourage struggled over the dunes just as the first split splat of rain made mini indentations in the sand.

By the time they reached the old estate car they were damp and bedraggled. If the car had been a golden coach they would not have been more pleased to see it. It obligingly accommodated them all, their unlovely luggage and quite a lot of the beach. The windscreen wipers worked overtime on the way home.

* * * * *

'Sorry I'm late,' Reg said, when he arrived home. 'Had a good day dear?'

Jane was flopped in an armchair. 'Took the children to Southsands and we had a picnic. It was a nightmare and I'm exhausted. The car's in an awful mess – and it also stinks of fish and chips and vinegar, which we got on the way home. Yours is in the oven, by the way,' she added apologetically. Reg grinned in his usual good-natured way.

'Sounds as if you need a drink – here. How did Sally cope?'

Jane accepted her glass of wine gratefully. 'Well she still hasn't said anything, but I think that she enjoyed paddling in the sea. The rest of the day was enough to make her more mute that ever!'

'Poor little mite – we just need a breakthrough,' Reg said, leaning over the back of the chair and kissing Jane's forehead, 'Where's everyone now – its very quiet?'

'De-sanded, fed and hopefully asleep. I'll just go and check up on them.'

The baby was dead to the world, sprawled in his cot like an exhausted puppy, Ben had gone to sleep with his personal stereo tinning away in his ears, which Jane gently removed and Anna was sleeping with her two favourite bears who had no doubt been told all about the seaside. Jane thought that Sally was asleep too, but when she bent to kiss her, two thin arms sprouted out from the duvet and clasped her tightly around her neck.

'It was my very bestest day!' Sally whispered.

27 ~ The Red Car

The small Indian town was bathed in heat. Dust swirled from the road and dogs slept in patches of shade. It was market day. Everyone came out to the market and there was a buzz of activity and colour. The stalls, sheltering under their makeshift canopies displayed a large variety of wares and stallholders were loudly extolling their virtues.

People were looking, talking, laughing, haggling, poking at vegetables, smelling spices and herbs and holding garments up against themselves wondering if they would fit.

Rani had come to the market with his elder sister. Rani was nine, brown and lean and lively. His large dark eyes missed very little and he had a wide grin which, into play took over the whole of his face. At the moment, however he was not grinning. His sister had met a friend and they were talking. And talking. He ground little holes in the dust dry road with his sandals until his sister told him to stop.

'You go on and have a look at the stalls,' she said. 'I'll see you in a while.'

Rani scampered off happily and began to wander from one stall to another. He loved the atmosphere at the market – the sound of music emanating from various directions, the smell of spices, herbs, fruit and vegetables and food being cooked in large flat pans under somewhat precarious conditions. He was dazzled by the sparkling beads, bracelets and rings, he tinkled a skein of bells until told to stop by the stallholder. He thought how wonderful his mother would look in some of the saris, he stood, fascinated watching the snake charmer. He walked on, past carpets, pots and pans, shoes, bags and caged birds.

He then came to a stall which tumbled about with all sorts of things – ornaments, nuts and bolts, paper lanterns, toys, books, cooking pots – anything one could think of, some things were well used, others new. Then he saw, nestling between two tarnished cow bells, the nicest, smartest and shiniest toy car that he had ever seen. It was bright red, trimmed with silver and had black tyres. It looked brand new. Rani wanted that car more than anything he remembered wanting for a long time. The owner of the stall was leaning up against an awning post, smoking. Rani asked him how much the red car was – which was a pretty useless exercise as he had precisely nothing in his pockets. He looked longingly at the car once more and decided he had better go back to his sister.

His sister was still where he had left her –still talking to her friend - except that now they were giggling uncontrollably. What strange things sisters are Rani thought as he rushed up to her.

'Susha, Susha!' he cried, pulling at her skirt, 'there is a lovely, lovely red car on one of the stalls – do you think there is enough money to buy it? Oh! please Susha, PLEASE!'

'Of course we haven't enough money to buy cars, Rani – don't be so silly. We mightn't even have enough to get all the things on the list Mother has given us. I'm coming shortly – you take Mother's list and go and get the spices and herbs that she wants – there will be enough money in this purse for those.'

Rani took the list and the purse and made his way disconsolately back to the market stalls, still thinking about the red car. Oh! how he would love that car!

A small crowd had gathered around the spice and herb stall by this time and Rani wondered how long it was going to be before he was noticed. He was just in the process of trying to squeeze himself nearer the front of the crowd when his sharp eyes saw something very bad. A man quite near to Rani reached into the bag of a lady standing next to him, took her purse and hid it under a garment he was carrying over his arm. It was a quick, deft movement but Rani, from his low vantage point saw it quite clearly.

The thief then started to manoeuvre himself out of the crowd. But so did Rani who was smaller and quicker and by the time the man was half walking, half running away, Rani was alongside. He and his friends at school were past-masters at tripping each other up and Rani had no difficulty in suddenly running very close to his quarry and tangling up with his legs. The man let out a surprised cry as he fell hard in the dust and the purse shot out of his hand. Rani snatched it up, shouting, 'This man's a thief – he took a lady's purse!'

There followed a commotion, but Rani ran back to the spice stall and gave the purse back to its owner, who was suitably delighted and tipped a generous number of rupees into his hand.

By the time Rani returned to his sister she was at last saying goodbye to her friend. His eyes were shining and a grin covered his face. Clutched in his hands he had several small plastic bags containing spices and herbs. But in one bag there was a bright red car.

28 ~ The Fire

She fumbled the key out of her handbag and opened the front door. She saw it on the mat as soon as she entered the house. The letter. It was from him.

She had not heard from him during the last three long weeks. She felt a familiar little thrill in the recognition of his handwriting, even before she dropped her assorted parcels in a heap on the floor, picked up the letter and took it into the living room.

It was a gloomy early winter evening, and the room, on its own all day, felt cheerless. In the grate the fire waited to be lit. Cold, dark and lifeless, it had been waiting all day – waiting to dominate and transform the room with its warmth and its movement.

She had laid it before leaving the house in the morning – not just, she knew for her own comfort and convenience. It was also because he might come, as he sometimes did, without letting her know – 'to give her a nice surprise.' The fire added welcome and cosiness – so she wanted it to be ready. Before she sat down with the letter she drew the curtains and then struck a match and gave life to the fire.

She sat in the armchair fingering and savouring the letter, like a child looking forward to a treat. The fire popped and crackled, the flames that had fed on the burning paper now attacked the wood and slinked through the blackness of the coals. The white smoke curled and twisted as it was dragged into the darkness of the chimney.

She opened the letter. It was not the kind of letter which she had hoped for or expected. It was tender. It was tactful. It was final. It was an 'end of an affair' sort of letter which has been written for centuries by people who wish to avoid a face to face trauma.

Many tears have been shed over such letters – and now she added hers to the flow. Her tears ran unchecked down her cheeks and smudged the wretched words of the letter trembling in her hands.

The fire burned brightly now, causing shadows to dance to and fro in the dimly lit room. To her the fire was a blur of orange and red as everything else in her world went black and the words of the letter wounded over and over. For quite a long time the fire and the tears were all that moved in the room. Then, slowly and deliberately, she crushed the letter into a tight ball and put it on the fire. Just for a moment it was cradled amongst the coals, and then the flames investigated it, surrounded it and then consumed it, until all that remained were fragments which floated gently upwards like charred thistledown.

Cradled, consumed, destroyed – just as she felt herself to be. Then she reached for a framed photograph on a nearby table. Almost ceremoniously she removed the photograph from the frame and put it, too on the fire. The handsome smiling face glowed in the fire's light and then it became curled, twisted, grotesque as the flames surrounded it and it was blackened, burnt and gone.

Gone. She thought bitterly about how he would Phoenix away – on to pastures new, or back to the life that he had only said he had left, and in which she had no part. He would be all right – this was his choice – but not hers. How would life be for her, now?

She jabbed the poker into the fire and fed it with a log. There was hissing and spluttering as the log was accommodated on the coals and bright yellow flames crept over it She sat and watched as the flames grew bigger and the shadows in the room danced higher. The flames became smaller and still she sat.

Then the telephone rang and yanked her back to the here and now. Perhaps it was him?

Perhaps he was ringing to say that the letter was an awful mistake, written in a moment of madness? Perhaps everything would be all right after all?

Half in hope she picked up the telephone, cleared her throat and tried to speak as normally as possible.

'Hello?' It was not him. She found it difficult to keep the disappointment out of her voice. There was a lot of background noise going on which sounded as if the caller was in a pub. 'Who's speaking?'

'Sally?' the voice crackled, 'It's Simon, Simon Groves.'

'Oh Simon – what a surprise – I thought you were in the States!'

'I was – for two years. Came back a couple of weeks ago. I'm here in your neck of the woods visiting my sister. I wondered if you are free whether you could come and have a bite of supper with me?'

She did not feel at all like going out for supper. She would not be good company. She just wanted to nurse her misery on her own. She started to make some excuse about having a lot to do.

'Oh! – come on Sally – I'm only here at The Phoenix pub – its not far from you is it? At least come and have a drink with me – It'd be good to see you!'

'At The Phoenix – how very appropriate!'

'What do you mean?'

'Oh – nothing – just that it's quite – er – near.'

'See you then? In about half an hour?'

'OK. thank you – look forward to seeing you after all this time.'

'Great! Bye for the moment!'

She put the phone down thoughtfully. Why, she asked herself, should she not Phoenix too – literally if not metaphorically? Anyway, it might cheer her up a bit and take her mind off things just a little. How extraordinary that he should ring her just tonight. Not a a bad old stick, Simon.

She showered, put on a favourite casual outfit and repaired her face. The front door slammed.

Of the letter and the photograph there was no trace, and the fire, untended, shrugged and settled further down into the grate. If it had had a heart it would have known that its task for the day was done and it could die down content. As it was, its embers merely winked and glowed in the empty room as the shadows ceased to dance.

29 ~ Returning

Ella parked her car in a side street and walked slowly along the road until she came to the house. There it stood, smarter now, but familiar still, after thirty five years.

She had always sought to suppress the memories of the time that she was here – she was told it would be best. But how could she forget? It was the only time and in the only place that they had been together – a precious togetherness, tangled with confusion and hurt, love and exquisite tenderness and a parting of desperate and helpless sadness.

The house was not called 'Greystones' any longer. 'Rowan Grange', the neatly painted board near the gate announced, 'A Nursing Home of Quality.'

She made no attempt to resist the urge she had to walk up the drive. Memories sprang out at her with every step. It was a warm spring day. Daffodils, tulips and forget-me-nots jostled together in well-kept borders and empty seats basked in sunshine in the garden. The drive curved round to the side of the house, where the main entrance door was situated. She sat on a seat opposite – she could be a visitor – just coming, or going – or waiting.

She looked at the big old house. The original building now bristled with extensions and additions. There was an ambience of good order. The large main door gleamed gloss paint and was enclosed in a glass porch. The once pot-holed drive was widened and neatly gravelled and there was a ramp covering the shallow steps to the entrance. Green and gold painted signs arrowed to 'Visitors Car Park', 'Staff Only', 'Deliveries', etc. But the changes did not hide the familiar, and the years rolled back as if they had never been, between the then and the now.

She fingered the letter in her pocket. It was the letter which had made her come. An inexplicable decision in a way, but she felt that by being here again, the only place that they had shared, would help her to decide, finally, what to do about the letter.

With the soft spring sunshine on her face, she closed her eyes and let the memories flood over her as she had never let them before. She didn't resist them or hold them back, but allowed them to surround her, envelope her – faces, sounds, smells, emotions. Many remembered details surprised her in their coming, as they had been stored away for so long.

* * * * *

She was only sixteen and still at school. Some time after a Christmas party and a frantic, fumbling sexual skirmish with one Mick Rogers, the dreadful truth dawned on her. She was pregnant. In those days unmarried motherhood was not at all easily accepted, and was a 'respectable' girl's worst nightmare.

She had told Mick one afternoon, walking home from school. He was kicking a stone along, first with one foot and then with the other. When her news penetrated, he stopped, staring at her, white-faced, letting the stone roll into the gutter.

Why ever should she remember that, she wondered in her musing, about the stone?

Mick had found his voice to ask, unbelievingly, 'You sure?' 'Yes, or else – I wouldn't be telling you.'

'What ya gonna do?'

'Don't know.' Hot tears had trickled.

'Oh God! – I'm sorry, Elly. At least he didn't try and deny he was responsible.

'I really didn't mean – Oh God! – what about your folks?'

'It'll be awful – I think Mum may suspect, by something she said yesterday – but anyway – they'll know soon enough. Its too late to do anything but have it, because I've read about it in a medical book – abortions and things.

'Oh God!' was all Mick could say yet again, aghast.

She remembered looking at him, at his round, good-natured , boyish face, his tousled hair and his ink-stained fingers – and suddenly she had felt so much more responsible and mature than he.

'Mick, I won't tell it was you, I swear – no one can make me, and there's no point – you can't be a dad –not now – you just can't.'

He was too honest to be able to hide the look of relief on the face he turned to her, although he made an effort at protestation. She hoped that now he did have a nice family. He would be a good kind father, she thought.

That evening she had gone with her mother to see the doctor. It had not been a good experience.

Her parents were predictably horrified about the situation. They were 'Very disappointed in her.' 'Whatever will everyone think?' 'Such a disgrace!' 'What sort of parents do you think this makes us feel?' 'We shall have to try and keep it from Grandma Ferguson – what a good job it will all be over by the time she comes to visit in the spring.' 'No sixth form for you now!' ' *Why* won't you tell us who the father is? Why should he get off scott free?' 'The baby will have to be adopted, of course. The best thing will be for you to go away somewhere, where we can visit you, and when this business is done with, we shall have to put it behind us and get on with our lives again.'

She could hear their voices still, and the anguish and misery they caused her.

Her feelings were more mellow now. Her parents were of their time, and very upset.

The 'Moral Welfare Worker' had an office up a lot of stairs in a rather gloomy building. She remembered sitting with her mother in front of a kindly prim lady. Whilst her mother wept spasmodically, arrangements were made for her to go to a Mother and Baby Home until the birth, and then to stay there, looking after the baby for some weeks, until it was placed with adoptive parents.

She herself did not cry. She felt like a bewildered pawn in a nightmare game, too deeply unhappy for helpful, therapeutic tears.

She looked up now at the big entrance door and thought of the summer day when, paint peeling, it had swung open to admit her mother, herself and her suitcase.

Life at the Home was more tolerable than she had expected. The staff were strict but on the whole, caring, and there was the companionship of the other girls. Fellow travellers along the same road form a bond whilst they journey together, irrespective of their starting points or their destinations when their paths cross no more. She remembered some names – Pam, Jackie, Doreen, Val – and wondered what Life had held in store for them – and their babies. They all had to work quite hard at the Home – cleaning, helping in the kitchen and coping with seemingly endless laundry.

A large conservatory had been built in the area where the banners of white nappies used to billow on long lines. She could almost hear the girls laughing, the staff scolding – and the babies crying. Almost the whole of their interest centred around babies – pregnancy, childbirth and baby care – and some of them were not much more than children themselves.

Her baby girl had been born in a haze of fear and pain and eventual triumph. But what she was totally unprepared for was the overwhelming and all-consuming love she felt for the tiny helpless new person she had produced. She could feel her softness even still, the down of her hair and the perfection of her fingers and toes. She called her Rosie – a little flower.

Helped by the staff, she had quickly become competent at baby care and for the next few weeks she was in a little cocoon of happiness, looking after her baby, loving her and not thinking about the tomorrows. Then one day she was asked to dress Rosie in her nicest clothes. When she was ready a member of staff came and took her gently away, to hand her over to the adoptive parents who were waiting in another room. She never saw or heard of her again. The following day she remembered tearful goodbyes and waiting forlornly in the hall with her suitcase, for her mother to come and take her home.

Shortly afterwards her father gained a promotion. She recalled, not without a little resentment, how thankful the family were to move to another area. The baby episode was never mentioned. If only they had let me grieve a little, she thought now, as she remembered the lonely nights when she had cried herself to sleep. My baby was not just something to be ashamed about and not to be mentioned – she was beautiful and a person and mine and I loved her – and I had to give her away. She thought of the one keepsake she had of Rosie which she had secretly kept, carefully wrapped in tissue paper – a tiny pair of white silk shoes, each adorned with a pink rosebud.

The memory of having her baby taken away came as vividly to her now as if the events which had spawned it had occurred days rather than decades before. She let it fill her whole consciousness, reliving the acute sense of grief and loss, anger and helplessness.

Somehow, in doing so, she felt a sense of release and almost of healing. She was heedless of the tears which were running down her cheeks.

An elderly lady, walking in the garden with the aid of a stick, gently touched her shoulder as she passed by.

'You must have had a bereavement, my dear – I'm so sorry,' she said, kindly. Ella managed a grateful smile, accepting the sympathy expressed which was so unknowingly belated – and the first she had ever had for the loss of her baby.

She began to think more positively. She thought lovingly of her good kind husband and her two fine sons. After the birth of her second son she remembered someone had burbled about 'how nice it would have been to have had a little girl this time.'

'I have a daughter,' she had allowed herself to think – 'somewhere.'

She thought of Rosie now – not as a baby, but as a woman, perhaps with a family of her own. She thought of Mick Rogers, and with difficulty tried to imagine him as anything but a rumpled-looking schoolboy. She wondered if he ever thought about her and the baby he had so haphazardly fathered.

She fingered the letter in her pocket again. It was not written in overt terms, but it said enough for her to know that Rosie had taken steps to find her. Her heart leapt to think of it. The ball was in her court – but she must be quite sure that her decision is right – right not just for herself, but for everyone. She thought of her family – John and the boys, and of her now very elderly parents. She had told John about Rosie very early on in their relationship and he had been nothing but understanding – but that is different from him being confronted by an adult step-daughter! And how would the boys react to an instant, much older half-sister? What if Rosie – or whatever she may be called now – is disappointed in her if they met, or angry about her rejection? What about her possible family – her adoptive parents, a husband, children? Would they really want her, Ella, materialising from the past?

Her thoughts went to and fro, as they had done since she received the letter. Here she could freely remember, grieve, decide. As she sat in the familiar, yet unfamiliar garden, her priority became very clear. She had an overwhelming desire and need to see her daughter, who must feel the same about meeting her. With love and understanding other problems would be overcome. Meeting each other would end a sense of incompleteness for them both. It would give her the joy of telling Rosie that she had never forgotten her, that she had always loved her, that she had not rejected her, but had been given no choice but to part with her. And she would hold her again!

She left the garden and as she walked down the drive she looked back at the house with a strange sense of gratitude. She knew that once again she had no choice – no choice about her answer to the letter.

30 ~ The Christmas Cat

She was cold and hungry. She toured round the farmhouse, her paws making little indents in the light layer of snow. She mewed outside the kitchen door and jumped up on the kitchen window sill. Sometimes these ploys gained her admittance into the house, with the bonus of a tit bit or a saucer of milk. Then she could often find a comfortable place in which to curl until the dogs disturbed her or she was shooed outside again by Him or Her or by one of the Smaller Hectic People. Her place was Outside, like any good farm cat. In this way she had to justify her existence by controlling the rodent population in the barns.

The trouble was that she liked it better Inside with the people and the comfort. She liked it when someone stopped and stroked her or rubbed her under her spotless white chin. She liked it when she was given something to eat which she hadn't had to stalk and catch for herself. She liked it when she was able to sneak Inside by the wood-burning stove when there was no warm sun outside.

Today, however, it was hopeless. There were no interesting smells wafting around for her to sniff, no lights or faces at the windows, no sound. There was a small tree which had suddenly grown inside the house with small shiny things dangling from it which she would very much have liked to investigate with a paw, but the window in front of it was very firmly closed.

She padded back across the yard to the apple barn. All was quiet. Even the dogs were nowhere – not that she was too sorry about that. She prowled around the barn. No mouse obligingly scurried about or squeaked in alarm at her presence.

She shook her paws, fluffed out her tortoiseshell coat and made a decision. She would seek comfort Elsewhere. She left the farmyard and skirted along the edge of the fields and into unfamiliar territory.

* * * * *

Mrs Consumed-with-good-works Havering-Brown helped Marjorie out of the car.

'I'm so pleased that you were able to come to our Christmas Eve lunch at the Golden Oldies Club, Marjorie, I do hope you enjoyed it.'

'Yes indeed, it was very nice, and thank you for providing the transport.' said Marjorie.

'That's been my pleasure,' the just slightly patronising voice answered, 'now just let me help you up the path – we don't want to slip, do we?

Marjorie felt that as the answer to that question was obvious it did not warrant a verbal reply. She fumbled her keys from her handbag and opened the door.

'Would you like to come in for a moment?'

'Just to make sure that you are settled – but I can't stay as have just about a million things to do!'

'Yes, I'm sure that you must be very busy. It was good of you to give your time to the lunch today.'

Mrs Havering-Brown followed Marjorie into the sitting room. 'Oh, it's the least I can do for people on their own – so sad, at Christmas. What are you doing tomorrow? Are none of your family coming?'

'No, my son is on duty at the hospital, so even his family won't see much of him and my daughter has gone to the States to spend Christmas with her in-laws. She didn't really want to go as it is our first Christmas without my husband, but it was all arranged and I insisted that they went.'

'Christmas isn't quite the same without the family is it?' was the well-meant but not particularly tactful response. Would you like me to make you a nice cup of tea?'

'No thank you – unless you have time to stay for one yourself?'

'Oh, I must fly. Now you look after yourself – and perhaps you would like to come to the Golden Oldies Bingo in the New Year? I'll see myself out. Bye now! Happy Christmas!'

The good lady bustled off and with a guilty feeling of relief Marjorie heard the front door close. She went to the mantelpiece and lovingly fingered the photograph of the man who smiled out at her. 'Oh Robert, is it too ungrateful of me to feel that I never want to go to the Golden Oldies ever again? It wouldn't be your cup of tea either. But people are kind – even if some of them think that if you are on your own and 'getting on a bit' you are therefore somewhat simple-minded, hard of hearing, unable to see properly and likely to fall over. She smiled at the photograph and wrinkled her nose. 'I do miss our chats and our laughs Robert – talking to your photo is a bit one way – but it helps. Anyway, I'm not going to sit and feel sorry for myself this strange Christmas. I shall think about all the Christmases we've had of course – but in a positive way – we've had them and nothing can take them away. But it feels strange not to have anyone else to – well – to care about. However, I'll go and put the kettle on – that's always a good thing to do.'

* * * * *

The little cat was beginning to feel alarmed. The last field she had skirted had led to a lane and then into a road trafficked by fast vehicles the like of which she had never encountered before. There were a lot of hurrying people about and music playing and little lights everywhere. twinkling and blinking. She went through a hedge into a garden but this set off a cacophony of dog barking which made her scramble to the top of a fence and stay there, fluffed out in alarm until the dogs were called away. Then she ran down out of the garden to a quieter place away from the frightening traffic and near some more fields. She came to another house and crept round it. There were lights on and a face at a window. She sat and licked a paw. If in doubt, wash.

* * * * *

There is, thought Marjorie, something very comfortable about warming a teapot in readiness to make some tea in it. It felt good to hold the nice round shape in your hands and swoosh the hot water about inside. Just as she picked up the boiling kettle she thought that she heard a soft mewing sound